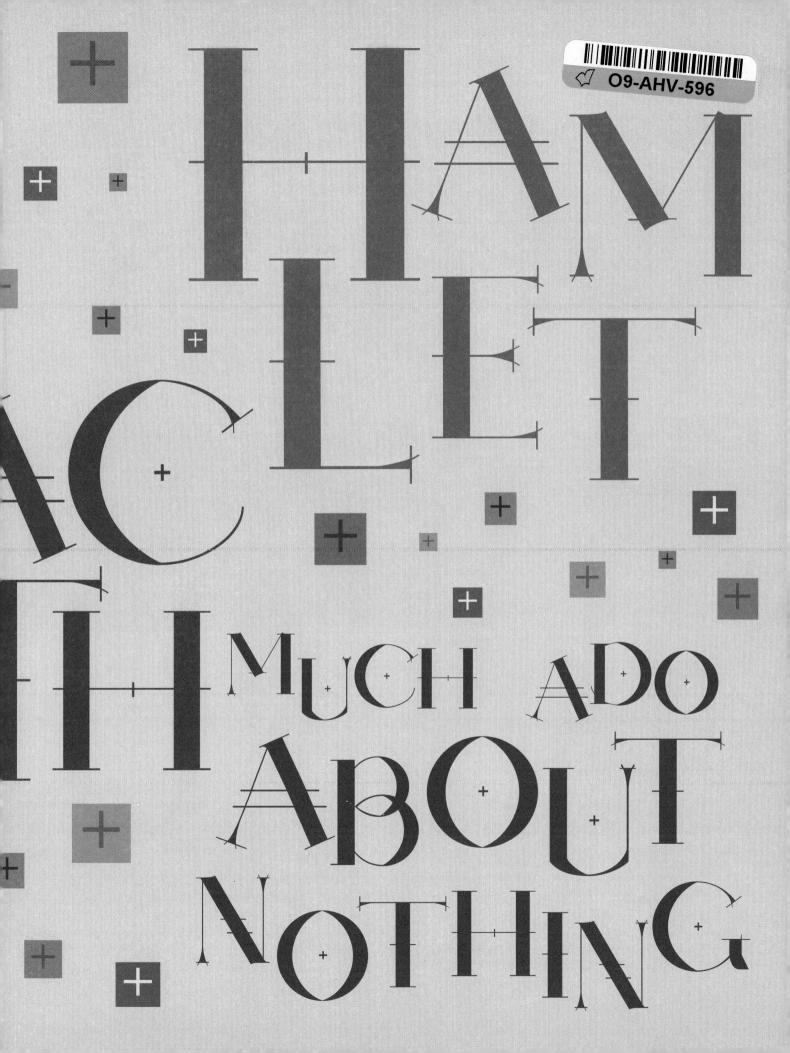

HAMLET

MUCH ADO ABOUT NOTHING

TALES FROM
SHAKESPEARE

RETOLD BY TINA PACKER

ILLUSTRATED BY

GAIL DE MARCKEN · LEO AND DIANE DILLON

MARY GRANDPRÉ · P. J. LYNCH · BARBARA McCLINTOCK

CHESLEY McLAREN · BARRY MOSER · JON J MUTH

KADIR NELSON · DAVID SHANNON · MARK TEAGUE

SCHOLASTIC PRESS · NEW YORK

TO KEVIN COLEMAN, MARY HARTMAN, AND THE ARTISTS WHO
WORK IN THE SCHOOLS FOR SHAKESPEARE & COMPANY. — T. P.

LIBRARY OF CONGRESS CATALOGING-IN-PUBLICATION DATA

Packer, Tina, 1938-   Tales from Shakespeare / by Tina Packer ; illustrated by Gail de Marcken . . . [et

al.].   p.   cm.   Summary: A collection of prose retellings of ten familiar Shakespeare plays, each illus-

trated by a well-known artist or artists. Contents: A midsummer night's dream / illustrated by Gail de

Marcken — Hamlet / illustrated by P.J. Lynch — Much ado about nothing / illustrated by Mary GrandPré

— King Lear / illustrated by Leo & Diane Dillon — As you like it / illustrated by Barbara McClintock —

Macbeth / illustrated by Barry Moser — The Tempest / illustrated by Mark Teague — Othello / illustrated

by Kadir Nelson — Romeo and Juliet / illustrated by David Shannon — Twelfth night / illustrated by

Chesley McLaren.   ISBN 0-439-32107-7   Shakespeare, William, 1564-1616—Adaptations—Juvenile lit-

erature.   [1. Shakespeare, William, 1564-1616—Adaptations.] I. De Marcken, Gail, ill. II. Title.

PR2877.P33 2004   822.3'3—dc21

10 9 8 7 6 5 4 3 2 1   04 05 06 07 08   Printed in Singapore 46

First printing, April 2004 · Book layout by Kristina Albertson · Book design by David Saylor

CONTENTS

William Shakespeare's plays are more than 400 years old. What could a writer of the sixteenth century possibly have to say to us in the twenty-first century?

Everything.

Shakespeare wrote about us, about all-too-human human beings. He understood that on some level, nearly everyone wants the same thing: to feel love and compassion for others; to be loved in return; to eat, drink, and sleep in peace and safety; to survive in a larger world and to live a life that has meaning, a life that will somehow serve a greater good. Shakespeare also understood people are flawed and often fall short of their noble (or *ig*noble) plans. Shakespeare was a genius at showing us ourselves.

> *I could have stay'd here all the night to hear good counsel.*
> *O, what learning is!* — ROMEO AND JULIET

William Shakespeare was born in Stratford-upon-Avon, England, in 1564. His father owned a glove-making business. Shakespeare did not follow directly in his father's footsteps.

At that time, public schools for children had only just begun in England. Before then, most children didn't know how to read and write; they learned a trade or farmed. Shakespeare went to one of these new public schools as a boy. There he learned Latin, which was a language all educated people spoke, no matter what country

INTRODUCTION

they lived in. From London to Lisbon, from Alexandria to Constantinople, from Tunis to Jerusalem, educated people spoke Latin, as well as their native tongue. All important documents, whether state, church, or trade, were written in Latin.

Shakespeare also studied the works of writers and philosophers from ancient Greece and Rome. More than 100 years had passed since Johannes Gutenberg introduced the printing press to Europe in 1452. Shakespeare and other English people who could read—and afford—books became familiar with stories from places such as Italy, France, Asia Minor, and North Africa. Some of these stories became the basis for great Shakespearean plays. For example, Apuleius's *The Golden Ass*, an ancient story from North Africa, probably was one of the tales that inspired *A Midsummer Night's Dream*. Shakespeare borrowed the story for *Romeo and Juliet* from a fellow English writer, who got it from a French writer who translated the story from a sixteenth-century Italian tale by Luigi da Porta, who swore it was based on fact.

Who can control his fate? — OTHELLO

In Shakespeare's world, there was an accepted order of things. Almost everybody in England was Christian. There was a fairly rigid class system. At the bottom were laborers; above them were farmers and tradespeople; the class line then rose to the lower clergy and squires, then on up to knights, earls, archbishops, and dukes. The monarch was enthroned at the top of this social order. In England, that monarch was Queen Elizabeth I (followed by her nephew, James I).

Elizabeth I ruled England for most of Shakespeare's life. She was queen for forty-five years, from 1558 to 1603. (Having a queen on the throne didn't make life any freer for girls. They still received little schooling and were expected to stay home and help their mothers until they were married themselves. None of this was true for Queen Elizabeth, though. She was very well educated, spoke five languages, and never married.)

England prospered under Elizabeth I. There weren't any civil wars. The queen's diplomacy kept tensions between England's two rivals, France and Spain, in check. (The Spanish tried to invade a few times, but were driven off.) Trade flourished. London became a crowded, bustling, enterprising city. Playhouses were built in London; these theaters were very popular places to visit.

Some are born great, some achieve greatness, and some have greatness thrust upon them. — TWELFTH NIGHT

The class system of Shakespeare's time may have been ordered, but it wasn't static. People really began to think for themselves. Shakespeare lived during the Renaissance. *Renaissance* means "rebirth" and that's what went on in Europe from about the fifteenth through the seventeenth centuries.

Renaissance Europe was alive with a revival of classical learning. There was a surge of creativity and interest in art, music, and architecture. An old, somewhat stagnant world was giving way to a new, vibrant world. While most people believed that the position of the sun, moon, stars, and planets affected what happened to you in life, some people started to change the way they thought of themselves and the world they lived in. They began to understand that power and position were created, not decreed by God or birth. They realized that Christianity was not the only religion and that it could have things in common with Judaism, Islam, mysticism, and even pagan rites and rituals. They made connections between their childhood experiences and the adults they became. And because some people could now read for themselves, they didn't always want to stay in the class into which they were born. Many Renaissance adventurers set out to seek their fortunes and improve their lot in life. Shakespeare was one of them.

I grow, I prosper. — KING LEAR

In the early 1590s, William Shakespeare established himself as a playwright and actor in London. In addition to acting and writing, Shakespeare also owned part of the playhouse he and his company performed in. That's probably how he made most of his money.

Shakespeare's wife, Anne, and their three children, Susannah and the twins Judith and Hamnet, stayed behind in Stratford. Shakespeare most likely visited them once a year.

Shakespeare became a very famous, very popular, and very wealthy man of the theater. Queen Elizabeth I loved his plays; so did King James I, her successor. During his reign, Shakespeare's company became known as "the King's Men" because King James I was their special patron. Shakespeare and the King's Men performed at the royal court, as well as at the Globe theater, their playhouse, and the Blackfriars theater. To earn more money, the troupe also toured England, particularly during the plague years!

All the world's a stage . . . — AS YOU LIKE IT

Elizabethans didn't consider playacting or playwriting very respectable professions. And going to a performance at the Globe, or the other playhouses in London, was not like going to the theater now. It was more like going to a football game!

Elizabethan theaters were multileveled wooden buildings. The audience sat on three sides or stood in a pit on the ground floor. The center of the theater was open to the skies because there was no lighting. Thousands of people packed into the theater for the afternoon performances. Audiences shouted back at the actors. The Globe was a crowded, noisy, and *rowdy* place.

What's in a name? That which we call a rose, by any other name would smell as sweet. — ROMEO AND JULIET

The thousands of people who flocked to see Shakespeare's plays would have heard some of the 1,700 words he is said to have invented. Those words are still in use. For instance, if you **scuffle** with your sister, make a **deafening** noise that gives your mother a **splitting** headache, and she tells you to "**Hush! Hurry** up and go **downstairs**!", so now you feel **gloomy** and **lonely**, your prospects for fun **dwindle**, but a **gust** of wind blows the hair out of your eyes and suddenly your best friend arrives. You **embrace** your friend, and now see the **dawn** of a new day—you have used twelve words invented by Shakespeare.

You may wonder about some of the spellings in Shakespeare's plays and in these stories. Elizabethans spelled the way they talked. There was no "right" way to spell. You wrote a word the way you wanted someone to say it. If you were using "me" in a sentence, but really wanted to emphasize it, you would write "mee." If you wanted to shout it from the rooftops, you would write "Meee."

If you see the word "stayed" in a Shakespearean text, but it's spelled "stay'd," it's because Shakespeare wants you to say "stay'd" as one syllable, the way we pronounce it now. If Shakespeare had written "stayed," his actors would have said "stay-ed" (two syllables).

Unlike the Elizabethans, our spelling sometimes isn't always the same as our pronunciation. Sometime we have kept the spelling of a word from olden times, but its pronunciation has changed. For example, the word knight was once pronounced the way it is spelled k-ni-gh-t (4 syllables). If you try rolling these sounds around your mouth, you'll see how much richer the spoken language was then than it is now. In an oral culture, people put great detail into the tone, pitch, and sound when they spoke.

There was a uniform way of spelling in Latin. But Latin was merging with the Anglo-Saxon language spoken by English people in their everyday lives. These two languages—with a bit of French, because William the Conqueror from Normandy had invaded England in 1066 and become William I of England, and French was used to a great extent in the court and the laws—created the richness of what we call English today.

English is, of course, being used almost everywhere in the world today as the language of commerce. It changes all the time with new words being added from other languages or when we invent something new.

It is not enough to speak, but to speak true.
— A MIDSUMMER NIGHT'S DREAM

William Shakespeare wrote for twenty-five years, creating somewhere between thirty-six and thirty-nine plays that we know of. His topics ranged from comic romances to civil wars, from domestic

INTRODUCTION

romps to world-shaking political events. But underlying all of Shakespeare's dramatic works are three essential questions: What does it mean to be alive? How shall we all act? What must I do?

Shakespeare's plays offer some profound insights into these questions. That's why literary scholars study his work. It's why politicians turn to him for choice quotes. It's why philosophers find powerful new ways of thinking through reading and rereading his plays.

Studying Shakespeare is studying life itself, from all its different angles: psychological, political, philosophical, social, spiritual. The rhythm of his verse reflects the rhythms of the body—the heartbeat, the pulse, the breathing in and out—and becomes a heightened experience for both the mind and the body.

Acting in Shakespeare's plays onstage makes you very aware of how deeply you have to breathe so that your voice is strong enough for everyone to hear. Of course, not everyone gets to perform onstage. That's why I chose ten of Shakespeare's powerful plays to retell as stories here. I picked sad, tragic tales and funny, happy ones, so that you get an idea of the breadth and depth of William Shakespeare's imagination. I also chose stories that seem the most relevant to our day and age and deal with the problems you might face.

To be, or not to be, that is the question. — HAMLET

When you start thinking about Shakespeare's plays, or the retellings in this book, as handbooks for living, they make sense. If you use them to see parallels in your own world, to awaken your imagination, and open your mind and body to commit yourself to action, then your life will begin to shift. Open yourself up to the inspiration of Shakespeare. Be generous and assume other people are also generous. Express yourself, speak out, know when you are being manipulated, whether it's by your friends, your school, or the media. It's possible to think of the greater good while still taking care of yourself and those who are close to you. This is the true legacy of Shakespeare's plays—to see ourselves, to see the world, and to act. For to think deeply about things, to ponder and reflect and then laugh and play, is the essence of life. As Shakespeare himself said,

What a piece of work is man!

how noble in reason!

how infinite in faculty!

in form and moving, how express and admirable!

in action, how like an angel!

in apprehension, how like a god! . . .

— TINA PACKER

PRESIDENT AND ARTISTIC DIRECTOR,

SHAKESPEARE & COMPANY

LENOX, MASSACHUSETTS

INTRODUCTION

A Midsummer Night's Dream

"The course of true love never did run smooth." Nothing could be truer in *A Midsummer Night's Dream*! Sweethearts Hermia and Lysander are forbidden to marry. Demetrius is trying to woo Hermia, while Helena is fawning over Demetrius. Even the king and queen of the fairies are quarreling. And when the fairy king introduces an enchanted love potion, there's no telling who will fall in love with whom . . . or with *what*!

Illustration by Gail de Marcken

A MIDSUMMER NIGHT'S DREAM

THE MAIN PLAYERS

HERMIA, *a young noblewoman of Athens*

LYSANDER, *Hermia's beloved*

DEMETRIUS, *a young noble also in love with Hermia*

HELENA, *Hermia's oldest friend; in love with Demetrius*

OBERON, *King of the fairies*

TITANIA, *Queen of the fairies*

PUCK, *Oberon's mischievous messenger*

BOTTOM, *a weaver and would-be actor*

THE TIME & PLACE

ANCIENT ATHENS, GREECE

On tiptoe, Hermia barely reached Lysander's shoulders. But in all of ancient Athens, you could not find a more promising match. Petite Hermia was dark-haired and spirited. Lysander was handsome and steadfast. The two longed for the day that they might marry. But under Athenian law, a young woman's father chose her husband. And Hermia's father had chosen another suitor for her, Demetrius.

How Hermia wished that Demetrius had stayed in love with her best friend, Helena! Then poor Helena would not spend her days pining for Demetrius. And Hermia would not spend *her* days battling her bullheaded father.

When Hermia declared she would marry only Lysander, her father was outraged. He dragged her before Theseus, Duke of Athens, to demand justice. Lysander and Demetrius followed.

"As she is mine, so by our law I may dispose of her as I will," Hermia's father reminded the duke. "She shall go either to Demetrius or to her death."

Duke Theseus himself was soon to wed. His bride was Hippolyta, warrior queen of the Amazons. The marriage meant an end to the long battle that the Athenians and the Amazons had been waging. Theseus had ordered days of feasting, revels, and entertainment, all celebrating love. The duke wanted to help these young lovers. He didn't want Hermia's death upon his hands. But his duty was to uphold the law. Theseus could do nothing for Hermia and Lysander but suggest another option.

A MIDSUMMER NIGHT'S DREAM

A MIDSUMMER

A NIGHT'S DREAM

"Examine your feelings, fair Hermia," Theseus said. "Know whether, if you yield not to your father's choice, you can endure the life of a nun." Demetrius, the convent, or death—the choice was Hermia's. The duke told the young girl she had until his own wedding day to decide. Then Theseus, Demetrius, and Hermia's father left to tend to some business.

Hermia was devastated. Lysander cupped her hands in his. "Fear not, my love, the course of true love never did run smooth." He asked his beloved to meet him the following night in a nearby forest. Lysander proposed they steal away to his aunt's home, which was outside the jurisdiction of Athens. There, they could marry.

Hermia threw her arms around Lysander's neck. As the lovers embraced, Helena wandered in, aimlessly twisting a lock of her long golden hair. "Godspeed, fair Helena!" Hermia greeted her.

"You call *me* fair?" Helena sighed. "O, teach me how *you* look, and with what art you sway the motion of Demetrius' heart!"

Hermia glanced at Lysander. He nodded.

"Take comfort, Helena," Hermia said gently. "Demetrius shall no more see my face." She and Lysander told her about their plan to elope.

Helena wished her friends well. But after they were gone, the lovesick girl had a foolish idea. "I will go tell Demetrius of Hermia's flight. He will pursue her to the wood and I will follow him. If nothing else, I may gain his gratitude."

Now these four young Athenians were not the only ones whose hearts were in upheaval. Oberon, king of the fairies, was quarreling with his queen, Titania. The queen was raising a mortal boy whose mother had been her dear friend. Oberon wanted the child as his page. Titania, who doted on the boy, refused.

The very night that Hermia and Lysander fled to the woods, the royal fairy couple chanced upon each other in a forest clearing. They eyed each other coldly. The king's lip curled in a sneer.

"Ill met by moonlight, proud Titania. What are you doing here?" demanded Oberon. "Are you going to the wedding of your favorite, Duke Theseus?"

The queen lifted her chin. "What, jealous Oberon? Are you going to the wedding of *your* favorite, Queen Hippolyta?"

"Why should Titania cross her Oberon?" the king demanded. "I do but beg a little changeling boy to be my page."

"Not for thy fairy kingdom," Titania replied haughtily. She turned and led her fairy entourage back into the woods.

"Well, go thy way," Oberon called after her. But under his breath, he added, "Thou shalt not leave this grove till I torment thee for this insult." Oberon called for Puck, a mischievous sprite who was his most trusted servant. He told Puck where to find a flower that had once been pierced by Cupid's arrow. "The juice of it on sleeping eyelids laid will make a man or woman madly dote upon the next live creature that it sees," Oberon explained.

A MIDSUMMER NIGHT'S DREAM

Puck flew off in search of the magic plant. The king would use it to punish his queen. Suddenly, Demetrius burst into the clearing, followed closely by the stumbling, breathless Helena. Knowing that fairies are invisible to people, Oberon moved closer to observe this peculiar pair.

"Pursue me not," Demetrius shouted over his shoulder. "Do I not in plainest truth tell you I do not and cannot love you?"

"And for that truthfulness do I love you the more!" Helena lifted her long skirt and thrashed through some brambles. "Spurn me, but let me follow you."

Demetrius glanced around the clearing. "I'll run from you and leave you to the mercy of wild beasts!" he shouted. Demetrius made a break for a thick patch of trees. Helena sprinted after him.

Oberon stared after the couple thoughtfully. Just then, Puck returned and presented him with a small purple flower. Oberon tore off a few petals and gave them to Puck. "Seek through that grove," he said. "There, a sweet Athenian lady is in love with a disdainful youth. Anoint his eyes, but do it when the next thing he sees may be the lady. Thou shalt know the man by the Athenian garments he has on."

"I'll put a girdle around the earth in forty minutes," boasted Puck. And he sped away.

Oberon himself hurried to a thyme-covered bank where Titania often spent the night. He waited as her attendants played sweet music to lull her to sleep. Then he crept forward and squeezed the enchanted flower juice into the queen's eyes. The king laughed and whispered, "Wake when some vile thing is near!"

Not far away, Hermia and Lysander struggled through dense undergrowth. When they finally emerged into a clearing, they stopped.

"I have forgotten our way," Lysander admitted. He suggested they rest until daybreak. Hermia collapsed on a patch of moss and Lysander lowered himself beside her. Hermia blushed and asked her sweetheart to lie farther off—after all, they were not yet married. Lysander laughed awkwardly and found a spot some yards away. Soon they were both deeply asleep.

Shortly after, Puck flitted by in search of Oberon's disdainful Athenian youth. When he spotted Lysander, he smiled. "Who is here? Clothes of Athens he doth wear." The sprite quickly circled the clearing and spied Hermia. "And here the maiden, sleeping sound, on the dank and dirty ground." Puck knelt over Lysander and squeezed the magic flower juice into the young man's eyes. His job done, the sprite flew off to join Oberon.

Close by, Helena searched vainly for Demetrius, who had finally outrun her. She stumbled upon Lysander lying on the ground, and gasped. Demetrius had vowed to kill Lysander. Helena knelt over the still figure. Was he dead? "Lysander, if you live, good sir, awake!" she cried.

Lysander's lids fluttered open; his charmed eyes fixed on

A MIDSUMMER NIGHT'S DREAM

Helena. Passion turned his heart inside out. "Not Hermia, but Helena I love," he declared, seizing her hand. "Who will not change a raven for a dove?"

Helena's eyes filled with tears. It was hard enough to endure Demetrius's scorn. Now Lysander mocked her with false words of love. Helena twisted out of his grasp and plunged into the undergrowth. Lysander bolted after her with barely a backward glance at Hermia, who still lay sleeping.

Meanwhile, Puck looked for Oberon near Titania's forest bed. But before the sprite found his king, he found a new entertainment —and a chance for mischief! A band of local workmen had met in the woods to rehearse a play. They hoped to stage it for the duke's wedding feast. The workmen called their play "The Most Lamentable Comedy and Most Cruel Death of Pyramus and Thisbe." As actors, these workmen *were* most lamentable! And worst of all was a bombastic weaver named Bottom who played the part of the romantic lead. Puck was thoroughly amused by Bottom and the other men enthusiastically blundering through their lines. He decided to add his own mischievous magic to the comedy—by topping Bottom with a donkey's head.

When the donkey-headed weaver made his next stage entrance, the other men shouted in alarm, "O monstrous! O strange! We are haunted!" The terrified men scattered. Puck barreled after them, intent on a good chase.

Unaware of his transformation, Bottom decided his friends were playing a joke on him. "This is to make an ass of me," he said. "To fright me if they could." In defiance, Bottom started singing loudly, to prove he wasn't afraid. His dreadful braying woke the fairy queen. When Titania laid eyes on Bottom, the enchanted flower juice worked its magic.

"What angel wakes me from my flowery bed?" Titania exclaimed. She appeared before Bottom. "I pray thee, gentle mortal, sing. Mine ear is much enamored of thy note." Titania tenderly caressed Bottom's long furry jaw. "So is mine eye enthralled by thy shape."

Bottom was amazed by the beautiful fairy queen's attention. But as she twined her arms around his shaggy neck, he shrugged happily. "To say the truth, reason and love keep little company together now-a-days," the weaver said and chuckled. His laugh sounded like a donkey braying.

Having chased Bottom's fellow workmen to the edge of the forest, Puck was resting against a tree when Oberon found him.

"How now, mad spirit?" the king greeted him. "Has my queen awakened?"

Puck's eyes twinkled. "Titania with a monster is in love!" He told Oberon of the queen's passion for foolish Bottom.

The king laughed. "This falls out better than I could devise. But hast thou yet bathed the Athenian's eyes with the love juice?"

A
M
I
D
S
U
M
M
E
R

N
I
G
H
T
'S
D
R
E
A
M

"That is finished, too," Puck said.

The sound of human voices echoed through the forest. It was Hermia, still desperately searching for her missing love, Lysander. But all she had found was the loathsome Demetrius. Hermia was sure he had done something terrible to Lysander.

"Stand close," Oberon said to Puck. "This is the same Athenian."

Puck's lip twitched in merriment. "Nay, this is the woman, but not this the man."

"Why do you rebuke him that loves you so?" Demetrius was pleading.

"Where is Lysander?" Hermia cried. "It can only be that thou hast murdered him, otherwise he would be here."

"I am not guilty of Lysander's blood," Demetrius protested.

"Well, see me no more, whether he be dead or no," Hermia answered. And with that, she fled.

Demetrius collapsed on a bank. "There is no use following her when she speaks so fiercely." He leaned back and closed his eyes.

Oberon looked sternly at Puck. "Thou hast mistaken quite and laid the love juice on some true love's sight," he said. "About the wood go, swifter than the wind, and find Helena of Athens," the king commanded.

As Puck disappeared, Oberon anointed Demetrius's eyes with the enchanted flower juice.

Puck quickly returned. "Helena is here at hand, followed by the youth mistook by me. Now will two at once woo one. Lord, what fools these mortals be!"

Lysander was indeed close on Helena's heels. "Why do you think that I woo in scorn?" he entreated her.

Helena, blinded by tears, nearly tripped over Demetrius. The young man awoke. As soon as his eyes focused on Helena, he reached out for her. "O goddess, nymph, perfect, divine!"

Helena was thunderstruck. "Now you both vow, and swear, and super praise my parts, when I am sure you hate me with your hearts."

Lysander placed his hand upon Helena's arm and looked at his rival. "Demetrius, with all good will, in Hermia's love I yield you up my part. My heart now belongs to Helena."

Demetrius scrambled to his feet and took Helena's other arm. "Lysander, keep thy Hermia; if ever I loved her, all that love is gone."

Lysander's voice drew Hermia into the clearing. She watched the scene with mounting disbelief. "Lysander, you speak not as you think; it cannot be!" She turned to Helena. "You thief of love! What, have you come by night, and stolen my love's heart from him?"

"Ah, so, now I see," Helena cried. "You are one of this confederacy! Will you ruin our friendship to join with men in scorning your dear friend?"

Hermia saw how Helena's willowy figure complemented Lysander's tall, lean form. "Are you grown so high in his esteem because I am so dwarfish and so low?" she wailed, dropping to her

A MIDSUMMER NIGHT'S DREAM

knees. "I am not yet so low but that my nails can reach into thine eyes." Helena fled into the woods.

Puck let out a hearty laugh. "Their jangling I esteem a sport."

As their own quarrel deepened, Lysander and Demetrius drew their swords. Demetrius gestured toward a nearby clearing.

Oberon turned to Puck. "You seest these lovers seek a place to fight. Therefore dim and overcast the night. Lead these testy rivals so astray as one come not within another's way." The king produced a sprig of herb, an antidote for Puck to squeeze in Lysander's eyes when the angry suitor stopped to rest. Leaving Puck to his labor, Oberon went off to find Titania.

Puck led the young Athenians on a merry chase through the darkened woods. He spoke first with Demetrius's voice, goading Lysander in one direction. Then he flew to Demetrius and egged him on using Lysander's voice. The men grew weary; at last Puck brought them to a clearing, to rest near each other. He drew Hermia and Helena to that spot, too. As the foursome slept, Puck anointed Lysander's eyes with the herb he got from the king. The sprite sang, "Now Jack shall have Jill; naught shall go ill; and all shall be well."

Puck went to report to his master. The king was spying on Titania and Bottom. A magnificent crown of flowers encircled Bottom's donkey ears. The foolish weaver was having a grand time ordering around the queen's fairy attendants. He sent one to fetch him honey and made another two scratch his shaggy head. "I must to a barber's, for methinks I am marvelous hairy about the face," Bottom declared.

As Titania curled herself around Bottom and they fell off to sleep, the queen declared, "Oh how I love thee! How I dote on thee!"

Oberon produced another sprig of the herbal antidote. "I do begin to pity her," he admitted to Puck. The king explained that he had met Titania earlier and taunted her about her love for the donkey-headed mortal. She had begged his patience and readily given up the human child he wanted as his page. Now, Oberon crept forward and squeezed the herb into the queen's eyes.

When Titania awoke, her passion for Bottom seemed like a hazy dream, and her love for Oberon was rekindled. At the king's command, Puck removed the donkey's head from Bottom, who slept on blissfully. The royal fairies and their followers then fled before the sun rose.

Dawn brought Duke Theseus's wedding day. He and his bride led an early morning hunting party, which included Hermia's father. As they rode through the wood, Hermia's father spotted his daughter asleep on the ground—alongside Lysander, Demetrius, and Helena. He was outraged.

"Is this not the day that Hermia should give answer of her choice?" Theseus asked him. The duke ordered his huntsmen to waken the foursome with their horns.

Lysander tried to explain how they came to be there, but

Hermia's father cut him off. "I demand justice!" he cried. "They would have stolen away! I say Hermia must marry Demetrius."

Demetrius scrambled to his feet. "My lord," he appealed to the duke. "I know not by what power, but my love for Hermia has melted as the snow." He reached for Helena's hand and helped her up. "Now the object and the pleasure of mine eye is only Helena."

Hermia looked at Lysander uncertainly. She'd had such a vivid dream about losing his love. But Lysander's gaze was steadfast and loving. And who could fault a person for how he behaved in a dream? Hermia reached for Lysander's hand; they rose together.

Hermia's father opened his mouth to protest, but Theseus silenced him. It was the duke's wedding day, and he had made his decision. "I will overbear your will," he told Hermia's father. "In the temple, side-by-side with us, these two couples shall eternally be knit."

Lysander lifted Hermia into the air and kissed her. Helena melted into Demetrius's arms. Hermia's father sputtered in anger, but he couldn't disobey the duke.

That day, amidst much fanfare, the three couples were married in the temple. The feasting and merriment lasted late into the evening—the merriest moments provided by Bottom, the workmen, and their "Lamentable Comedy."

At midnight, the duke's servants snuffed the candles and the newlyweds went up to bed. Sly Puck crept into the castle. Oberon and Titania soon followed with their fairy band. They sent their sprites to bless the lovers and all the castle's inhabitants. The fairy king and queen themselves blessed the bridal bed of Theseus and Hippolyta. Then Titania and Oberon clasped hands and joined together in their own dance of eternal love:

Hand in hand, with fairy grace,
Will we sing, and bless this place.

HAMLET

"Something is rotten in the state of Denmark." The king has died mysteriously. His widow has married his brother. The king's ghost haunts the royal castle. He wants his son, Hamlet, to avenge him. A sensitive, questioning soul by nature, Prince Hamlet now swears to take his violent revenge—a vow that will cost him dearly.

Illustration by P. J. Lynch

31

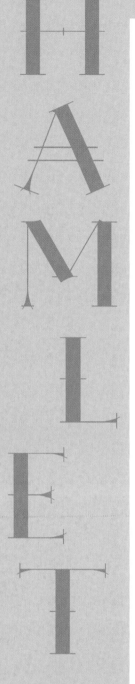

THE MAIN PLAYERS

HAMLET, *Prince of Denmark*

KING CLAUDIUS, *Hamlet's uncle*

QUEEN GERTRUDE, *Hamlet's mother*

HORATIO, *Hamlet's friend*

POLONIUS, *the king's chief counselor*

OPHELIA, *Polonius's daughter*

LAERTES, *Polonius's son*

THE TIME & PLACE

HUNDREDS OF YEARS AGO, DENMARK

Prince Hamlet of Denmark paced the

torch-lit battlements atop Elsinore castle. The clank of weapons being forged echoed from the dungeons below. Laughter and music floated up darkened passageways. A royal feast was being celebrated. But Hamlet had no appetite for festivities. He was seeking graver company—his father's ghost!

Hamlet's friend Horatio had the night before in this same place seen a ghostly figure dressed in royal armor. The prince had ample reason to believe that the spirit of his kingly father might be restless. Hamlet's mother, Queen Gertrude, a widow but four months, had married Claudius, the new king and her dead husband's brother. Meanwhile, Prince Fortinbras of Norway threatened to invade Denmark. These were uneasy times in the late king's kingdom!

A cannon blast sounded below, signaling that Claudius had just drunk another toast to his new wife. A fresh wave of melancholy washed over Hamlet. "How weary, stale, flat, and unprofitable seem to me all the uses of this world," he said aloud. "'Tis an unweeded garden. Things rank and gross in nature possess it."

Suddenly, a chill filled the air. A figure appeared, shrouded in fog. It moved soundlessly, though it was clad in warrior armor. The figure beckoned to Hamlet.

"List, list, oh list," a hollow voice called forth from the figure. Its visor stood halfway up. Hamlet saw the ghostly image of his father's black-and-silver beard!

HAMLET

HAMLET

"I am thy father's spirit," the ghost declared. "If thou didst ever thy dear father love, revenge my foul and most unnatural murder."

"Murder?" Hamlet cried.

"Murder most foul," the ghost answered. "'Tis given out that, sleeping in my orchard, a poisonous snake did sting me," the ghost continued. "But know, thou noble youth, the serpent that did sting thy father's life now wears his crown."

"O my prophetic soul!" Hamlet cried. "My uncle!" It was Claudius who had poured deadly poison into the king's ear.

"Ay, that beast, who with witchcraft of his wit, won to his shameful lust the will of my most seeming-virtuous queen." The ghost's armored fists clenched. "Swear to revenge my murder," the ghost hissed.

Hamlet fell to his knees before his father's spirit. "I swear, I swear!" he cried.

"Let not thy soul contrive against thy mother," the ghost continued. "Leave her to heaven, and to those thorns that in her bosom lodge to prick and sting her."

The eastern sky grew light. Dawn was coming. The cock crowed and the ghost faded. "Adieu, adieu," it called. "Remember me."

"Remember thee?" Hamlet raised his sword, swearing a vow. "In thy commandment all alone shall I live."

As Hamlet descended into the castle, he considered what he must do. The code of honor demanded that he kill his uncle, the new king.

The only fitting way to avenge his father's murder was to kill his father's murderer. But Hamlet was a student, a thinker, not a warrior like the old king. He would have to conquer his own sensitive temperament to do this bloody deed. And Claudius was a crafty observer of human nature. He would quickly recognize Hamlet's intent. Troops were already amassing in the castle because of the threat from Norway. With a snap of his fingers Claudius could increase his own force of palace guards, making Hamlet's task maddeningly impossible.

Inspiration slowed Hamlet's steps. What if he put on a show of madness, such as sometimes befalls a person under great strain? That would allow him to stay near the king without arousing suspicion. No one but Horatio need know Hamlet was in his right mind.

In another part of the castle, the young Lady Ophelia stood with her father, Polonius, the king's chief counselor. They were bidding farewell to her brother, Laertes, who was returning to France. The chief counselor had some wise advice for his son.

"Give every man thy ear, but few thy tongue," Polonius told Laertes. "Neither a borrower nor a lender be. And this above all: to thine own self be true. My blessing with thee."

His son dispatched, Polonius turned a critical eye on Ophelia.

"What is between you and the prince Hamlet?" he demanded.

Ophelia blushed. She and Hamlet had grown up together, and she had loved him for as long as she could remember. "He hath, my lord, of late made many tenders of his affection to me."

"Affection! Pooh! You speak like an immature girl." Polonius frowned. Didn't Ophelia realize that a prince could not marry for love? He must marry a princess, not a commoner like Ophelia. "I would not," Polonius pronounced, "from this time forth, have you spend any moment's leisure as to talk with Hamlet."

Ophelia loved Hamlet desperately. But she dared not defy her father. She blinked back tears. "I shall obey, my lord."

From then on, Ophelia spoke not a word to Hamlet. With great regret she returned his letters unopened. She sometimes heard whispering in the palace about the prince, tales of strange conduct and nonsensical speeches. But she could not appear to be too interested, nor could she allow herself to get close enough to observe him.

One day, while Ophelia was sewing in her room, Hamlet burst in. His face was as pale as his shirt, and she thought he looked as if he had escaped from hell. He grabbed her by the wrists and wordlessly searched her face for a long minute. Then he backed out of the room, his sorrowful eyes never leaving hers.

Terrified, Ophelia ran to her father and told him all.

Polonius stroked his long white beard. "Have you given him any hard words of late?"

Ophelia shook her head. "As you did command, I repelled his letters and denied his access to me."

"That hath made him mad," Polonius declared. "Surely this is the very ecstasy of love."

Puffed up with self-importance, Polonius carried Ophelia's story to Claudius and Gertrude, for the king and queen were anxious to know the cause of Hamlet's strange behavior. With the royal couple's permission, Polonius set a trap to determine if Hamlet's mad behavior sprang from love denied. He commanded Ophelia to sit reading in a gallery where Hamlet often wandered. Polonius and the king stood within earshot, hidden behind a tapestry wall hanging.

Hamlet soon entered the far end of the gallery. Thinking himself alone, he reflected aloud on life's injustices. "To be, or not to be: That is the question: Whether 'tis nobler in the mind to suffer the slings and arrows of outrageous fortune, or to take arms against a sea of troubles, and by opposing end them?" This was the painful heart of Hamlet's dilemma. Perhaps it would be better to just die himself. "To die, to sleep; to sleep! perchance to dream. For in that sleep of death, what dreams may come. Ay, there's the rub. But that the dread of something after death puzzles the will, and makes us rather bear those ills we have than fly to others that we know not of." Hamlet became so tangled up in his own philosophizing, that he no longer knew which thoughts applied to himself. His confusion clouded his plans.

Someone entered the gallery. Hamlet saw it was Ophelia. He was stunned and delighted. In his recent display of madness, he had paced the entire castle a dozen times a day, but never once had he seen her outside her private chamber. Hamlet quickened his steps.

Ophelia's eyes flicked involuntarily to one side. Hamlet spied

HAMLET

two pairs of polished boots beneath a wall hanging. His heart sank. It was bad enough that Ophelia had been refusing his letters. Was she now helping the king spy on him?

Hamlet fixed her with a cold stare. "Where's your father?"

"At home, my lord," Ophelia stammered.

"Let the doors be shut upon him," Hamlet shouted, "that he may play the fool nowhere but in his own house!" Leaning close, he added, "Get thee to a nunnery. Or if thou wilt marry, marry a fool. For wise men know well enough how you betray them." With one more look at the wall hanging, he bid Ophelia farewell and ran from the room.

Ophelia was frightened by the prince's mad outburst. She dissolved into tears. "O! What a noble mind is here o'erthrown," she wept. "Woe to me, to have seen what I have seen, see what I see."

Claudius emerged, shaking his head. "Love? His emotions do not that way tend. There's something in his soul o'er which he broods."

Later that day, a troupe of traveling actors arrived to perform for the Danish royal court. Hamlet greeted them eagerly, happy to spend an hour thinking about something other than his father's murder. After the players retired for the night, Hamlet's thoughts returned to revenge. But once again, confusion reigned in the prince's mind and he had second thoughts.

"The ghost that I have seen may be the devil in a pleasing shape," he considered. "I'll have proof more convincing than its words. I have heard that guilty creatures sitting at a play have been

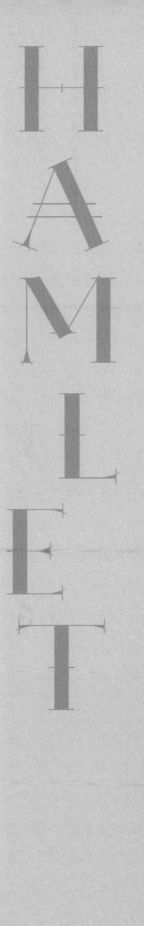

struck so to the soul that they have proclaimed their crimes. I'll have these players play something like the murder of my father before mine uncle. If he but flinch, I know my course." Hamlet smiled. "The play's the thing wherein I'll catch the conscience of the king!" The prince rushed off to find the actors and instruct them as to what play he wanted them to perform.

The next evening, the royal court assembled for the players' performance. The first scene began with assurances of love between a king and queen. The king lay down for a nap in his garden, and his queen left the stage. Another actor entered, playing a relative of the king. The actor uncorked a bottle of dark liquid and poured it into the king's ear.

Claudius leaped to his feet. "Give me some light!" he yelled. Servants rushed toward him with flaming torches, but he barreled through them. "Away!" he cried and fled the room, Gertrude and Polonius close behind.

Hamlet elbowed Horatio. "Didst thou perceive?"

"Very well, my lord," Horatio agreed.

The queen summoned her son. Savoring his small victory, Hamlet climbed the stairs to his mother's private room.

Meanwhile, Claudius, alone in his chamber, wrestled with his conscience. "My offence is rank, it smells to heaven—a brother's murder!" The king sank to his knees and clasped his hands together. "Help, angels!"

Just then, Hamlet passed the king's bedroom. He saw Claudius kneeling, unguarded and unarmed. Hamlet eased his sword out of its scabbard and crept up behind the king. He raised his weapon to strike. Now, he might do it!

"But he is praying," Hamlet reflected. "If now I do it, so he goes to heaven. A villain kills my father, and for that I do this same villain send to heaven?" He shook his head. "I'll do it when he is drunk asleep or about some act that hath no relish of salvation in it." The prince lowered his blade and slipped quietly out of the room.

Claudius struggled to his feet, frowning. He had not been able to pray after all. He repented the murder, but not the crown and queen it had brought him. "My words fly up, my thoughts remain below," he sighed. "Words without thoughts never to heaven go."

Frustration whetted Hamlet's anger at his mother. He strode into her chamber and grabbed her by the shoulders. "You shall not budge till I set up a mirror where you may see the inmost part of you."

Gertrude had never seen this wild look in her son's eyes. "What wilt thou do?" She felt Hamlet's grip tighten. "Thou wilt not murder me? Help!"

"What, ho! Help! Help!" A man's muffled voice came from behind one of the queen's wall hangings.

Hamlet pushed his mother away and drew his sword. He rushed at the wall hanging. "How now! A rat?" With a swift thrust, he pierced the cloth—and whomever lay behind it.

"Oh what a rash and bloody deed is this!" Gertrude cried.

"Almost as bad, good mother, as kill a king, and marry with his brother," Hamlet replied.

"As kill a king?" Gertrude's mind flashed on Claudius's reaction to the play.

Hamlet pulled aside the slashed wall hanging. The bloody corpse of old Polonius slumped forward. "Thou rash, intruding fool," said Hamlet. "I took thee for thy better." He had imagined it was Claudius spying there.

Gertrude faced her son uncertainly. "What have I done that thou wags thy tongue in noise so rude against me?"

Hamlet reached for her throat in answer. Gertrude gasped. The prince removed her locket, which held a painting of Claudius. From his own neck, he produced a locket with the image of his father. He dangled it before her. "This was your husband. See what grace was seated on this brow." Hamlet held up his mother's locket. "Look you now what follows. This is your husband: a murderer and a villain."

Gertrude shuddered.

Hamlet suddenly released his mother's locket. He stared, transfixed, at the doorway in which his father's ghost now stood. "Do you come your tardy son to chide?" he asked the ghost.

"Do not forget," the ghost replied. "This visitation is but to whet thy almost blunted purpose."

H
A
M
L
E
T

Gertrude followed Hamlet's horrified gaze . . . and saw nothing. "Alas!" she whispered. "He's mad!"

The ghost faded and Hamlet turned back to his mother. "Repent what's past," he said. "Avoid what is to come."

Gertrude studied the portrait in her locket. "O Hamlet! Thou has cleft my heart in two."

"Then throw away the worser part of it, and live the purer with the other half." Hamlet stood. "Good night; but go not to mine uncle's bed."

Gertrude snapped her locket shut and buried her face in her hands.

Polonius's murder gave Claudius a powerful excuse to banish Hamlet. He ordered the prince to sail for England immediately. Claudius sent two of Hamlet's friends with him. They were also the king's spies; one of them carried a sealed letter to the English, requesting Hamlet's swift execution as soon as he arrived.

From her chamber window, Ophelia watched Hamlet depart. What should she make of this lover-turned-stranger who now eyed her so sadly? Hamlet was still the man she loved with all her heart. Yet he was also her father's killer, whom she must hate. As the days went by, this contradiction shattered Ophelia's heart, then splintered her mind. She wandered the castle as Hamlet had once done, but her madness was no ruse. She sang mournful songs and handed out wildflowers and sprigs of herbs.

Ophelia's brother, Laertes, sped back to Denmark at the news of his father's death. When he saw his sister, his grief doubled. "Is it possible a young maid's wits should be as mortal as an old man's life?" he cried.

Strange news reached the castle: Hamlet had returned to Denmark and was on his way back to court . . . *alone*. Claudius realized his plan had failed. He also realized that Laertes's anger might prove useful to him. Claudius told Laertes that Hamlet had killed Polonius. He reminded him that as a good son, he should avenge his father's murder.

Claudius convinced Laertes to challenge Hamlet to a fencing match. Instead of a blunted foil, the king explained, Laertes would substitute a sharpened one. Eager to avenge Polonius's death, Laertes produced a vial of poison in which to dip his sharpened sword tip. Claudius promised to serve Hamlet a goblet of poisoned wine for good measure.

As they were sealing these plans, the queen rushed in, distraught. "Your sister's drowned, Laertes!" Gertrude cried. Ophelia, carrying garlands of wildflowers, had climbed a willow tree that hung over a brook. As she reached to hang her decorations, a branch snapped and she slipped into the water. "Her clothes spread wide, and, mermaid-like, awhile they bore her up," Gertrude said. "She chanted snatches of old hymns, as one unknowing of her own distress. But long it could not be till her garments, heavy with their drink, pulled the poor wretch to muddy death."

Horatio, meanwhile, had gone to the port city to escort Hamlet home. En route, they passed Prince Fortinbras's Norwegian army. Hamlet admired the forceful prince who had struck a deal with Claudius and now marched forward to conquer other lands. Hamlet couldn't help but compare his own ambivalence and inaction with Fortinbras's spirited ambition. The time had come. "From this time forth, my thoughts be bloody, or be nothing worth!" Hamlet resolved.

As Hamlet and Horatio rode toward Elsinore, the prince told his friend the particulars of his escape. Hamlet described how he had secretly altered the sealed letter to order the deaths of his untrustworthy friends.

Hamlet and Horatio passed through a cemetery as they neared. A gravedigger was shoveling out an old grave to make room for a new corpse. The gravedigger unearthed a skull, which he showed to Hamlet. "This same skull, sir," he said, "was Yorick's skull, the king's jester."

Hamlet turned the skull around in his hands. "Alas! Poor Yorick. I knew him, Horatio. A fellow of infinite jest, of most excellent fancy." He smiled at the skull fondly. "Where be your gibes now? Your flashes of merriment?"

They heard somber music, such as heralded a funeral. Hamlet and Horatio hid themselves as a royal procession entered the gate.

"Who is that corpse they follow?" Hamlet whispered. The body, wrapped in plain cloth, was lowered into the earth. With a cry Laertes leaped into the grave, weeping and calling his sister's name.

Hamlet gasped. "What! The fair Ophelia?" He darted out of his hiding place. "I loved Ophelia!" he shouted. "Forty thousand brothers could not, with all their quantity of love, make up my sum." He too leaped into Ophelia's grave.

Laertes lunged at Hamlet, and the two men had to be wrested apart. Horatio swiftly led Hamlet toward the castle, while the king calmed Laertes by reminding him of their lethal plan.

The following day, the banquet hall was outfitted as a fencing ring. All the court came to watch the match. Hamlet and Laertes faced off. They circled each other warily. Then Laertes lunged, the poisoned tip of his foil pointed straight at Hamlet's heart. Hamlet batted the thrust aside. He turned and touched Laertes with his blunted sword tip.

"A hit," announced the fencing judge.

Pretending to celebrate Hamlet's successful strike, the king handed him a jeweled goblet—filled to the brim with poisoned wine.

Hamlet passed the cup, untouched, to a servant. "I'll play this bout first; set it by awhile."

The second round lasted longer. Hamlet moved quickly to parry Laertes's blows. The prince lunged three times before he finally landed a second hit on his opponent.

Gertrude rose to her feet. She took Hamlet's goblet from the

H A M L E T

servant's hand. The queen raised the cup: "To thy fortune, Hamlet."

Claudius reached out to stop her, but she had already drained half of the poisoned liquid. The king lowered himself onto his throne, stunned.

The sword fight resumed. In the third round, Laertes surprised Hamlet. He flicked his sword against Hamlet's arm. Its sharp tip cut a shallow wound.

Enraged, Hamlet turned on Laertes. He struck the illegal foil out of his grip. A scuffle followed. The prince grabbed the sharp sword and Laertes got the blunted weapon. In no time, Hamlet wounded Laertes with the poisoned foil. Both men now bled.

Suddenly, the queen gasped for air and tumbled from her chair. With horror, she realized that her son had been right about her husband. "Oh my dear Hamlet! Your drink! I am poisoned."

As Hamlet rushed to the dead queen's side, Laertes sank to his knees.

"Hamlet, thou art slain," Laertes called. "The treacherous instrument is in your hand." He shivered violently. "The foul practice has turned itself on me. The king, the king's to blame."

Hamlet stared at the sword in his hand. "The point envenomed, too? Then, venom, to thy work." The prince leaped at Claudius and ran the sword into his chest. He seized the jeweled goblet and poured the rest of the lethal wine down his uncle's throat. Twice poisoned, the king died swiftly. Finally, Hamlet had done the ghost's bidding.

Laertes drew his last breath. "Noble Hamlet!" he gasped. "Mine and my father's death come not upon thee, nor thine on me." The two wounded swordsmen forgave each other.

Warlike noises came from outside the hall. A courtier rushed in with news that Fortinbras and his Norwegian army were at hand. Hamlet staggered. The poison from the sword wound spread. The prince called for his one true friend. "Horatio, thou alone livest. In this harsh world draw breath to tell my story." Then Hamlet collapsed. "The rest is silence," he said, and died.

Horatio looked around him in anguish. A king, a queen, a brave nobleman, and a prince, all dead. Prince Fortinbras strode in amongst the chaos and boldly declared his claim to the Danish throne. Grief strickcn, Horatio knelt by his beloved friend's body. "Good night, sweet prince," he whispered sadly. "Flights of angels sing thee to thy rest." Hamlet had indeed avenged his father—but at a terrible price to all.

MUCH ADO ABOUT NOTHING

After beautiful Hero becomes engaged to dashing Claudio, the couple helps trick an unlikely pair of sweethearts into falling in love: Hero's sharp-tongued cousin, Beatrice, and a confirmed bachelor named Benedick. But while Hero and Claudio plan their lighthearted games, a jealous prince plots a darker deception that will stir up much ado about everything!

Illustration by Mary GrandPré

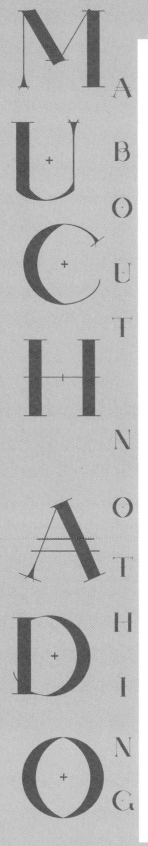

THE MAIN PLAYERS

LEONATO, *Governor of Messina*

HERO, *Leonato's daughter*

BEATRICE, *Leonato's niece*

DON PEDRO, *Prince of Aragon*

CLAUDIO, *officer in Don Pedro's army*

BENEDICK, *officer in Don Pedro's army*

DON JOHN, *Don Pedro's half brother*

THE TIME & PLACE

16TH CENTURY, MESSINA, ITALY

Hero; her father, Leonato; and her cousin Beatrice stood in front of the gates of the governor's palace. Hero gripped her father's arm tightly as a column of gallant officers on horseback neared. At the head of the column rode Don Pedro, a dashing prince who had led this army to victory in a recent small battle, one of the many clashes that broke out in Italy in those days. But Hero's eyes sought out the figure to Don Pedro's right—young Claudio of Florence, who had bravely distinguished himself in the fight. Hero smiled bashfully at her hero. Claudio smiled back at the young woman.

Beatrice looked coolly at the officer riding to the left of Don Pedro. It was Claudio's friend, Benedick of Padua.

The military column halted at the palace gate. Governor Leonato saluted them. With his permission, they would rest in his city before heading out to the next skirmish.

As Benedick dismounted, he returned Beatrice's contemptuous glare. "My dear Lady Disdain! Are you still living?"

"Is it possible Disdain should die while she hath such food as Signor Benedick?" Beatrice shot back.

Don Pedro introduced his half brother, the prince Don John, to Leonato. Don John was a disloyal brother and a melancholy soul. Still, Don Pedro had recently patched up his differences with his brother and wanted Don John to be accepted in society.

Governor Leonato ushered his guests inside. He gestured for his daughter and niece to follow.

MUCH ADO

ABOUT NOTHING

Claudio watched Hero disappear into the palace. "Benedick, didst thou note the daughter of Signor Leonato?" he asked his friend. "She is the sweetest lady that ever I looked on."

"I can see yet without spectacles, and I see no such matter," Benedick replied bluntly. He did not intend to admit that any woman was beautiful—or ever fall for any woman's charms.

"But I hope you have no intent to turn husband, have you?" Benedick asked Claudio suspiciously.

"If Hero would be my wife," Claudio admitted.

Benedick rolled his eyes. "Is it come to this?"

Don Pedro lingered at the palace door, waving at his officers to follow. "What secret hath held you?" he asked when they caught up.

"Claudio is in love with Hero," Benedick answered flatly.

Don Pedro clapped Claudio on the back. "Amen, for the lady is very well worthy."

Benedick sighed. "That a woman conceived me, I thank her. That she brought me up, I likewise give her most humble thanks. But *I* will live a bachelor."

Don Pedro laughed. "I shall see thee, ere I die, look pale with love."

"With anger, with sickness, or with hunger, my lord, not with love," Benedick swore.

That evening, Leonato hosted a victory celebration, a fancy dress ball. The ladies, decked out in their finest gowns, filled the hall with vibrant colors. The uniformed officers playfully disguised themselves with grotesque and gaudy masks.

Hero danced and laughed with Don Pedro, though she didn't recognize him. Beatrice, who smarted from her prickly encounter with Benedick, was now thoroughly enjoying herself. She whirled around the dance floor; one man after another gladly served as a foil for her lively wit.

During one dance, Beatrice found herself in the arms of a man whose nimble feet kept perfect time with her own. She peered curiously into the eyeholes of her mysterious partner's mask; the man retreated further into his disguise. He then remarked that he had overheard someone say Beatrice was arrogant, and that her witty sayings were merely repeated from a book.

Beatrice's cheeks glowed red. "It must have been Signor Benedick that said so," she guessed. "He is the prince's jester, a very dull fool." Beatrice spun away and took the hand of the next dancer.

Her mysterious partner left the dance floor. Out of Beatrice's sight, he slipped off his mask. It was Benedick. "The prince's fool!" he said. "Ha! It is the bitter disposition of Beatrice that so gives me out." Benedick tried to enjoy himself, but his eyes kept darting toward Beatrice.

The disgruntled officer was soon joined by Don Pedro and Leonato who had his daughter, Hero, in tow.

"I hear the Lady Beatrice hath a quarrel with you," Don Pedro

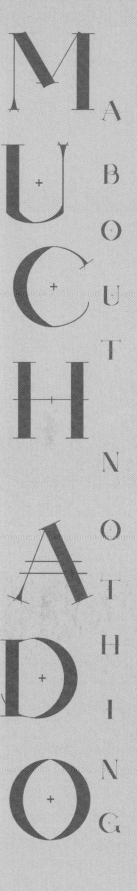

teased Benedick. "A gentleman that danced with her told her she is much wronged by you."

"She misused *me*!" Benedick fumed.

"Look, here she comes." The prince smiled at Beatrice, who was leading Claudio toward the group.

"Will your grace command me any service to the world's end?" Benedick pleaded. "I will fetch you a toothpick now from the furthest inch of Asia rather than hold three words' conference with this harpy." With a pointed look at Beatrice, he strode away.

"Lady, you have lost the heart of Signor Benedick," Don Pedro said solemnly, but his eyes twinkled.

"Indeed, my lord, he lent it me awhile, and I gave him interest on it—a double heart for his single one." Beatrice forced a light-hearted laugh. "No matter. I had rather hear my dog bark at a crow than a man swear he loves me."

Don Pedro shifted uncomfortably. He had forgotten that years ago, Benedick and Beatrice had briefly courted, but the romance had come to nothing. Perhaps that explained Beatrice's riddle of an answer and why she and Benedick had no civil words for each other. Of course, that could mean they still cared for each other. . . .

The prince reminded himself that there was another romance that clearly *had* blossomed: Claudio was smitten with Hero. The young lovers wanted to be betrothed. Don Pedro had spoken to Leonato about the whole affair and now brought happy news to his officer. "Claudio," the prince said, "fair Hero is won. I have obtained the good will of her father."

Leonato nodded happily in agreement. Overcome with joy, Claudio tenderly kissed Hero's hand.

Beatrice beamed as she hugged her cousin. "God give you joy!" she said to her cousin. Then, with a curtsy to the prince, Beatrice excused herself. In truth, she was saddened by all this romantic joy.

Don Pedro looked after her. "She were an excellent wife for Benedick."

"They would talk themselves mad!" Leonato laughed.

"I would gladly have it a match," Don Pedro insisted. He swore he could transform this pair of fighting gamecocks into lovebirds, if Leonato, Claudio, and Hero would help him.

All three merrily agreed.

Meanwhile, in a quiet side room, Don John sat brooding. He hated it when people were so happy. He especially hated Claudio, who held so much of Don Pedro's admiration and affection. "That young start-up hath all the glory of my overthrow," Don John complained to his servant Borachio, "and the Count Claudio shall marry the daughter of the governor."

"Yea, my lord, but I can thwart it," Borachio said. He revealed that he had been wooing Margaret, one of Hero's waiting women. Borachio swore he could convince Margaret to borrow one of Hero's gowns. Then he would trick her into speaking to him from Hero's window late at night. If Don John brought Claudio to witness this meeting, the young groom would surely think he saw his bride being unfaithful.

A smile flitted across Don John's surly face. "Be cunning in the working of this," he said, "and thy fee is a thousand ducats." Borachio raced off to find Margaret.

The next morning, Benedick strolled through the palace garden. He was avoiding Claudio, who talked only of Hero, Hero, Hero!

Just as Benedick settled onto a shady bench with a book, he spied Don Pedro, Claudio, and Leonato entering the other side of the garden. "The prince and Monsieur Love!" he groaned. "I will hide me in the arbor."

The three men pretended not to notice their friend dashing into the bushes. They ambled along to where they knew Benedick would be sure to overhear them.

"What was it you told me of today?" Don Pedro inquired loudly. "That Beatrice was in love with Signor Benedick?" Benedick's book tumbled to the grass. "Is it possible?" he whispered. On hands and knees, he scrambled to a better listening post.

"'Tis true indeed, so Hero says," Claudio replied. "Down upon her knees Beatrice falls, weeps, sobs, tears her hair, prays, curses, and cries 'O sweet Benedick!'"

"My daughter is sometime afeard she will do a desperate outrage to herself!" Leonato added, swallowing a smile.

"It were good Benedick knew of it," Don Pedro said.

"To what end?" Claudio asked. "He would make sport of it and torment the lady worse."

Don Pedro stepped closer to Benedick's hiding place. "I wish he would modestly examine himself, to see how much he is unworthy to have so good a lady," the prince said. "Beatrice is an excellent sweet lady, and she is virtuous."

"And she is exceeding wise," Claudio added.

"In everything but loving Benedick," Don Pedro corrected. With a wink, he led his companions out of the garden.

Benedick staggered to his feet, as disoriented as if the earth itself had shifted beneath him. "They say the lady is wise but for loving me," he whispered. "Indeed, it is no great argument of her folly, for I find I am horribly in love with her."

Meanwhile, Hero and her waiting woman Ursula had planted themselves in an orchard and tricked Beatrice into following them. She heard everything the two other women said.

"Are you sure that Benedick loves Beatrice?" Ursula asked.

"So say the prince and my new-betrothed lord," Hero replied. "But I persuaded them, if they loved Benedick, to urge him wrestle with his affection and never let Beatrice know of it."

"Why did you so?" Ursula asked, stifling a giggle.

"Disdain and scorn ride sparkling in her eyes, misprizing what they look on." Hero's own eyes sparkled with mirth. "Her wit values itself so highly that to her everyone else seems weak. She cannot

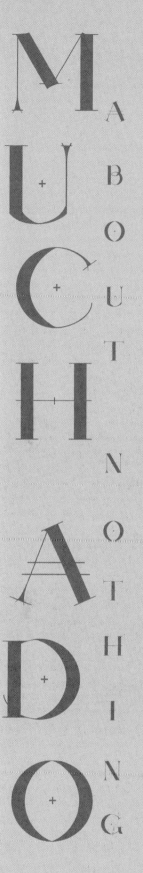

MUCH ADO ABOUT NOTHING

MUCH ADO
A BOUT NOTHING

love, she is so self-centered." The women agreed it was a hopeless cause and left the orchard.

"What fire is in mine ears?" Beatrice whispered. She knew her playful wit could bite, but she had thought it as harmless as a sharp-toothed puppy. She had never heard anyone but scornful Benedick chastise her for it. Perhaps she should look to herself and mend her ways. "Contempt, farewell! And maiden pride, adieu!" she vowed.

As for Benedick, should Beatrice once again trust this man? Her heart gave her the answer. "Benedick, love on," she said to herself. "I will tame my wild heart to thy loving hand."

That night, the men gathered together. Claudio and Don Pedro were in high spirits over their matchmaking. It was obvious that their ruse had worked: Benedick was serious of late. He wrote poetry. He was consumed by thoughts of love. He had even shaved his scratchy beard, no doubt out of concern for Beatrice's tender cheek!

Suddenly, Don John burst in upon the group. He swore he had proof that Hero was unfaithful. "Go with me and you shall see Hero's chamber window entered, even the night before her wedding day," the devious prince said. He was rewarded by the look of horror on Claudio's face. "If you love her then, wed her," Don John continued, "but it would better fit your honor to change your mind."

Claudio and Don Pedro followed Don John out into the darkness in disbelief. They were shocked by the scene before them: a woman leaning out of Hero's window, kissing another man!

Claudio burned with anger and humiliation. Now, he thought the angelic look on Hero's face seemed painted on; her sweet words earlier mocked. "In the congregation where I should wed, there will I shame her," Claudio vowed.

The wedding day dawned. When the ceremony was less than an hour away, the local constable pounded on the palace door, asking Leonato, as governor, to witness the examination of a prisoner. Leonato's mind was on his daughter's wedding. The constable's mind was equally scattered. He never thought to explain that his prisoner was Borachio, who had been caught bragging about tricking Claudio.

The governor shooed the constable away. "Take his examination yourself and bring it me," Leonato commanded.

A short time later, the wedding party stood before the friar in the chapel. Leonato joined his daughter's hand with Claudio's, but Claudio abruptly pushed Hero away. "What man talked with you last night betwixt twelve and one?" he demanded loudly.

The blood drained from the bride's face. "I talked with no man at that hour," Hero stammered.

Don Pedro stepped forward. "Myself, my brother, and this grieved count did see her talk with a ruffian at her chamber window." He looked at Hero scornfully. "And that vile man has confessed you have had meetings a thousand times in secret." Hero was speechless.

Leonato staggered. He would rather die than be dishonored by

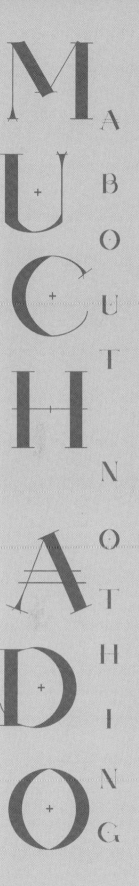

an unfaithful, lying daughter. "Hath no man's dagger here a point for me?" the governor cried.

Bewildered and terrified, Hero fainted into Beatrice's arms.

Claudio took an impulsive step in Hero's direction, but Don John held him back. The deceitful prince insisted that Hero had been overcome by a guilty conscience. He led Claudio out of the chapel.

Don Pedro followed and motioned for Benedick to join him. Instead, Benedick pushed by the prince and helped Beatrice ease her cousin to the floor.

"On my soul, my cousin is wronged!" Beatrice cried. She gently cradled her cousin's head; Hero's eyelids flickered open.

"Hence from her!" Leonato shouted. "Let her die!" He tried to tear Hero from Beatrice's grasp, but Benedick held him back. "O, she is fallen into a pit of ink," Leonato railed. "The wide sea hath drops too few to wash her clean again."

Hero weakly lifted herself onto her elbows. "My father," she begged, "if you prove that any man conversed with me at hours improper, refuse me, hate me, torture me to death!"

At last, the friar stepped in. He assured Leonato that he believed Hero to be innocent. Then he came up with a plan. "Your daughter here the princes left for dead," the friar said. "Publish it that she is dead indeed, and do all rites that apertain to a burial."

The friar predicted that when Claudio heard of Hero's death, he would be overcome with grief and remember how much he had loved her. Perhaps then he would reexamine his reasons for accusing her.

Not knowing what else to do, Leonato agreed. He and the friar led Hero to a hiding place, leaving Beatrice and Benedick alone in the church.

"Sure I do believe your fair cousin is wronged," Benedick said.

"Ah, how much might the man deserve of me that would vindicate her!" Beatrice cried.

"Is there any way to show such friendship?" Benedick asked.

Benedick looked at Beatrice—her face red with anger, her eyes full of bitter tears. How beautiful she appeared to him even now! "I do love nothing in the world so well as you," he told her. "Is not that strange?"

"It were as possible for me to say I loved nothing so well as you. But believe me not—and yet I lie not." Beatrice was confused. She closed her eyes. "I am sorry for my cousin."

Benedick took her hand and drew her close. "By my sword, Beatrice, thou lovest me," he said.

Beatrice could hold out no longer. "I love you with so much of my heart that none is left to protest," she said. The two lovers melted into each other's embrace.

"Come, bid me do anything for thee," Benedick said.

Beatrice's reply was out of her mouth before she had time to think. "Kill Claudio."

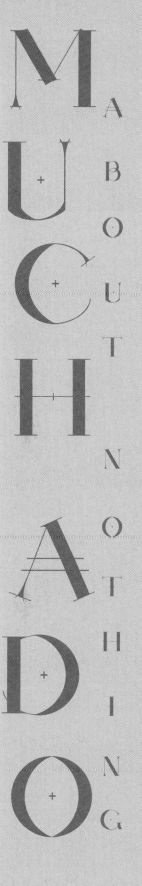

MUCH ADO ABOUT NOTHING

"Not for the wide world!" Benedick answered. His response was as swift as her demand.

Beatrice was enraged. First Hero was wronged, now Benedick reneged on his vow. "You kill me to deny it. Farewell," she said angrily. Beatrice twisted out of Benedick's grasp, but he wouldn't let her go.

"Think you in your soul the Count Claudio hath wronged Hero?" Benedick asked.

"Hath not he slandered, scorned, dishonored my kinswoman?" Beatrice answered. "O that I were a man! I would eat his heart in the marketplace."

"Enough, I am engaged," Benedick said quietly. "I will challenge Claudio to a duel."

That afternoon, Benedick found Don Pedro and Claudio preparing their horses for travel.

"We have been up and down to seek thee," the prince said, "for we are high-proof melancholy, and would gladly have it beaten away. Wilt thou use thy wit?"

Benedick's hand went to his sword. "It is in my scabbard," he replied. He grabbed Claudio by the collar. "Shall I speak a word in your ear?"

Claudio laughed hollowly. "God bless me from a challenge!"

"You are a villain," Benedick hissed. "You have killed a sweet lady, and her death shall fall heavy on you." He told Claudio to name the time and place they would fight.

Benedick then turned to Don Pedro. "My lord, I must discontinue your company. Your brother Don John is fled from Messina. You have among you killed an innocent lady." Benedick strode off.

Don Pedro stared after him. "Did he not say my brother was fled?" A moment later, the constable approached them, leading Borachio in chains. "How now, my brother's man bound?" the prince hailed. "What's your offence?"

Borachio bowed his head. "Don John paid me to slander the Lady Hero," the servant admitted. "You saw me court Margaret in Hero's garments."

As Don Pedro steadied the stunned Claudio, Leonato appeared, clutching Borachio's confession.

Claudio knelt before him. "Choose your revenge yourself."

Leonato pulled Claudio to his feet. He issued a strange punishment: "Tonight, go to the grave of Hero and ask for forgiveness. Tomorrow morning come you to my house. Since you could not be my son-in-law, be instead my nephew." He asked Claudio to marry a cousin of Hero and Beatrice, whom he said looked almost like Hero's twin.

Claudio sorrowfully agreed, though he could not imagine loving any woman other than Hero, no matter what she looked like.

The next morning, Leonato presented Claudio with a veiled stranger. Claudio tried to put aside his grief for this lady's sake. He took her hand. "I am your husband if you like of me."

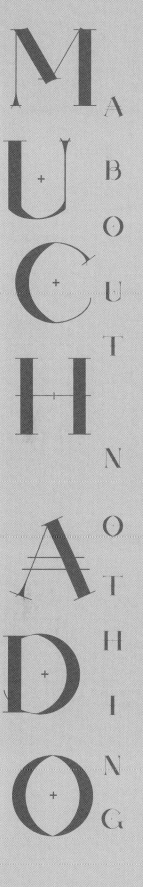

MUCH ADO ABOUT NOTHING

Hero slowly lifted her veil. "When I lived I was your other wife; and when you loved you were my other husband." She took Claudio's palm and pressed it to her cheek. Claudio embraced her gratefully.

"Hero that is dead!" Don Pedro cried.

"She died, my lord, only while her slander lived," Leonato said.

The friar beckoned the couple inside, but Benedick held the holy man back. "Friar, I must entreat your pains, I think." He turned to the woman at Hero's side. "Beatrice, do not you love me?"

Beatrice blushed at the amused stares of the assembled guests. "Why, no, no more than reason," she insisted.

"Why, then your uncle, and the prince, and Claudio have been deceived—they swore you did," Benedick said.

"Do not you love me?" Beatrice asked.

Now Benedick was embarrassed. "Troth, no, no more than reason," he swore.

"Why, then my cousin and Ursula are much deceived, for they did swear you did."

Claudio fished a piece of parchment from his pocket. "I'll be sworn upon it that he loves her, for here's a paper written in his hand, a halting sonnet fashioned to Beatrice." He placed it in Beatrice's palm.

Hero took a parchment from Ursula and delivered it to Benedick. "And here's another, writ in my cousin's hand, containing her affection unto Benedick."

The couple read the poems in silent wonder.

"Here's our own hands against our hearts." Benedick laughed heartily. "Come, I will marry thee, but only because I pity you."

"I would not deny you." Beatrice smiled. "But I yield upon great persuasion and partly to save your life, for I was told you were well-nigh dead for me."

"Peace! I will stop your mouth." And taking Beatrice in his arms, Benedick sealed her lips with a kiss. Then he looked at Claudio, Hero, and all assembled. "Come, come," cried Benedick joyfully. "Before we marry, let's have a dance to lighten our hearts! Strike up, pipers!" And so they did.

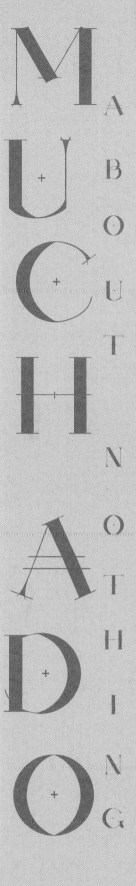

MAC+BETH

What happens when ambition turns evil? What happens when a man betrays his king, his friend . . . his own soul? Those questions are at the heart of *Macbeth*. "Fair is foul, and foul is fair" when the warrior-hero Macbeth and his wife aspire to become king and queen of Scotland. They think their only way to the throne is by the sword. But evil deeds have a way of revealing themselves. . . .

Illustration by Barry Moser

MACBETH

THE MAIN PLAYERS

MACBETH, *army general and Thane (baron) of Glamis*

LADY MACBETH, *Macbeth's wife*

DUNCAN, *King of Scotland*

MALCOLM, *King Duncan's oldest son*

BANQUO, *an army general*

MACDUFF, *Thane of Fife*

THREE WITCHES

THE TIME & PLACE

11TH CENTURY, SCOTLAND

Thunder crashed and rumbled across the barren Scottish heath. A lightning bolt silhouetted two men on horseback before the gloom swallowed them up.

"So foul and fair a day I have not seen," said Macbeth, Thane of Glamis. Banquo, the Scottish general who rode alongside him, silently agreed. Both men drove their horses forward across the windswept heath. They were bone-weary, but the exhilaration of victory raced through their veins. Macbeth's army had just crushed a bloody rebellion against Duncan, King of Scotland. Macbeth himself had slain the revolt's leader. Now Macbeth was anxious to reach King Duncan's castle—and whatever reward his service had earned him.

As Macbeth and Banquo neared the king's stronghold, three grotesque, rag-clad figures boiled up from the boggy ground. Startled, Macbeth reined in his horse before the strange beings. They were witches, said to possess wicked powers and foresee the future.

"All hail, Macbeth! Hail to thee, Thane of Glamis!" croaked the first witch.

"All hail, Macbeth! Hail to thee, Thane of Cawdor!" rasped the second.

The third witch gave Macbeth a jeering smile. "All hail, Macbeth, that shalt be king hereafter!"

Banquo pulled his mount even with Macbeth's. "If you can look into the seeds of time, and say which grain will grow and which will not," he charged the witches, "speak now to *me*."

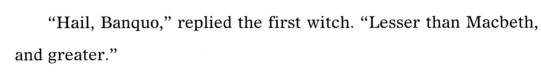

"Hail, Banquo," replied the first witch. "Lesser than Macbeth, and greater."

"Not so happy," added the second witch. "Yet much happier."

The third laughed aloud. "Thou shalt father kings, though you yourself be none."

Then the witches' garments began to grow misty and their skin transparent.

"Stay and tell me more!" Macbeth cried. He rode desperately into the creatures' dispersing mist. "By my father's death, I know I am Thane of Glamis," he shouted. "But how of Cawdor? The Thane of Cawdor lives."

Mist encircled the two generals like thick fog—and the witches were gone!

Macbeth looked at Banquo thoughtfully. "Your children shall be kings," he said.

"*You* shall be king," Banquo replied lightly.

Macbeth forced a smile. "And Thane of Cawdor, too. Said they not so?"

Suddenly, Banquo wheeled his horse around. "Who's there?" he shouted.

The sound of hoofbeats neared. Two riders emerged from the mist. They were nobles sent by King Duncan to escort Macbeth and Banquo to his royal castle.

One rider made a courtly bow. "The king bade us call thee

Thane of Cawdor," he told Macbeth. He explained that the former Thane of Cawdor had been found aiding the enemy. King Duncan stripped the traitor of his thane's title and bestowed it upon Macbeth.

As the messenger spoke, the color drained from Macbeth's face. He should have been overjoyed at his new title. He had earned it through his valiant service to King Duncan. Yet Macbeth thought only of the witches' prophecies. One had now come true.... Would the other? Would Macbeth someday take Duncan's place? And how might that come to pass? he wondered. The king was growing old. But he had two healthy sons, both in line for the throne. Was Macbeth meant to fulfill the witches' prophecy by his own hand—a hand clutching a dagger? The thane's own thoughts made him shudder. He spurred on his horse. "Let us toward the king," he said.

Macbeth, Banquo, and the two noblemen soon arrived at court. King Duncan announced a further honor: He would pay a royal visit to Macbeth's castle. Straightaway, Macbeth sent a letter to his wife so that she could make preparations. He also told her of the witches' strange prophecies.

When Lady Macbeth read her husband's letter, her heart beat wildly. Ambition flooded her whole being. King and Queen Macbeth! And why not? Both she and her husband were of royal blood. Lady Macbeth tapped the letter against her palm. "Yet do I fear my husband's nature," she reflected. "It is too full of the milk of human kindness." If they were going to rule Scotland, she must convince her husband to do away with Duncan. Tonight the king would sleep in their castle. What better time to end his reign . . . by taking his life?

With her entire being, Lady Macbeth reached out to the same dark powers the witches served. "Come you spirits that tend on murderous thoughts!" she cried. "Fill me from the crown to the toe, top-full of direst cruelty. Make thick my blood. Stop up all access to remorse, that no mercy or compassion may shake my fell purpose."

The door flew open. Macbeth rushed in, his eyes wild. He, too, had been thinking of murder.

"Your face, my thane, is as a book where men may read strange matters," his wife chided. "You must look like the innocent flower, but be the serpent under it." She calmed her husband and went to prepare for the royal party.

That night King Duncan and his entourage arrived to a warm welcome. At the huge feast, Lady Macbeth encouraged the king and his servants to drink a lot. When she noticed that Macbeth was missing from the party, she graciously excused herself and sought out her husband.

She found Macbeth pacing nervously. He looked at his wife with desperation. "We will proceed no further in this business," Macbeth said, "if we should fail . . ."

"Screw your courage to the sticking-place and we'll not fail," Lady Macbeth insisted. She relayed her plan: She had already mixed a sleeping potion into the wine Duncan and his party were so heartily enjoying. After the king retired to his bedchamber, Lady Macbeth would ply his grooms on guard outside the room with more of the laced wine. When the grooms passed out, she'd remove their knives and lay them out in plain sight. Then Macbeth could steal in and use those knives to execute the bloody business. Macbeth agreed. "I am resolved," he swore. He took himself off to dine with the king. "False face must hide what the false heart doth know," he warned himself.

After dinner, Macbeth grew restless. He paced outside in the courtyard waiting for Lady Macbeth's signal that all were asleep. As he walked, he beheld a disturbing vision.

"Is this a dagger which I see before me, the handle toward my hand?" he cried. Macbeth reached for the weapon, but caught only air. "I see thee still," he gasped, "and on thy blade great gouts of blood, which was not so before!"

The ghostly dagger disappeared just as a bell rang in the tower. It was Lady Macbeth summoning her husband to his bloody task.

"'Twere well it were done quickly," Macbeth said to himself. Before his courage flagged, he climbed the stairs to where the drunken grooms lay snoring. He gathered their weapons and crept into the king's bedchamber. A lamp still burned, but Macbeth dared

not look at Duncan's face. He took a deep breath and plunged both daggers into the king's chest. Then Macbeth fled to his own bed-chamber, still clutching the gory blades.

Macbeth burst into the room, where Lady Macbeth waited. "Why did you bring these daggers from the place?" she cried in panic. "They must lie there. Go carry them, and smear the sleepy grooms with blood."

"I'll go no more!" Macbeth insisted. "Methought I heard a voice cry 'Sleep no more! Macbeth does murder sleep!'" Macbeth was overcome by guilt. "Macbeth shall sleep no more," he wailed.

His wife grimaced. "Give me the daggers!" she hissed. Minutes later, Lady Macbeth returned, arms red to the elbows. "My hands are of your color, but I scorn to wear a heart so white," she said. She took her husband's bloody hands in hers. "A little water clears us of this deed," she said firmly.

Macbeth and his lady headed for their chamber. Daybreak came shortly after, along with a loud pounding on the castle doors. There stood Macduff, Thane of Fife. He had come to call upon his king. Macbeth greeted him. Macduff asked to be directed to his lord. Macbeth pointed out the way, and the newly arrived thane headed to the king's chamber.

He soon returned.

"Murder and treason!" Macduff shouted. "Ring the alarm bell."

Duncan's bloody body appalled all who saw it. Amidst the wailing and confusion, Macbeth and his wife put on a masterful show of grief. Then in a feigned rage, Macbeth even killed the drunken, bloodied grooms and called his act revenge.

Duncan's sons, Malcolm and Donalbain, feared that their own lives were in danger, too. They fled immediately, Malcolm to England and Donalbain to Ireland. Their departure drew suspicion: Had the princes paid the grooms to murder their own father? If not, why had neither son stayed to assume Duncan's throne?

A council of thanes met to name a new king. It did not take them long to decide: Duncan's crown was soon placed upon Macbeth's head. Now Macbeth and Lady Macbeth were King and Queen of Scotland. The witches' prophecy had come true!

But Macbeth did not revel in his success. He was wracked with suspicion and mistrust. He had murdered Duncan to gain the throne. What was to stop some other ambitious thane from trying the same evil deed?

Worse, Macbeth brooded over the witches' words to his friend and fellow general, Banquo. "They hailed him father to a line of kings—no son of mine succeeding!" Macbeth said bitterly. Macbeth and his wife had no children—and the witches had said nothing about *their* heirs.

"If it be so, for Banquo's children have I defiled my soul," Macbeth raged. "For them the gracious Duncan have I murdered!"

MACBETH

Macbeth resolved to take fate into his own hands once more. But this time he would work not to fulfill the witches' prophecies, but to defy them.

The newly crowned king arranged a royal banquet and invited all of Scotland's highest-ranking nobles. They celebrated his ascension to the throne. But Macbeth had another, darker purpose. The feast brought Banquo and his beloved only son, Fleance, into Macbeth's reach. As they approached the castle, Macbeth sent assassins to greet them. Banquo fell beneath their murderous blades, but in the confusion Fleance escaped.

The henchmen broke the news to Macbeth as his banquet began. His heart began to pound. With Fleance safe, the witches' prophecy could still come true. Macbeth tried to shake his unease. After all, Fleance was young. There was still time to take care of him, the king reassured himself.

Macbeth strode to the banquet table, which was full of exuberant noblemen. He raised a goblet and smiled at each man in turn. "Were the blessed person of our Banquo present," he said, "here would we have all our country's honored."

Suddenly, Macbeth's goblet tumbled from his hand. He stared down the long table. At its head sat a ghastly apparition crowned with blood—Banquo's ghost!

"Thou canst not say I did it!" Macbeth shouted at the crimson-haired ghost. "Do not shake thy gory locks at me."

The nobles began to rise. "His highness is not well," they murmured, for they saw nothing.

Lady Macbeth rushed to her husband's side. "Sit, worthy friends," she entreated. "My lord is often thus and hath been from his youth. The fit is momentary. If you note him, you shall offend him. Feed, and regard him not."

The queen pulled Macbeth aside. "Why do you make such faces?" she whispered.

"As I stand here, I saw Banquo murdered!" Macbeth insisted.

"This is but the painting of your fear," his wife hissed. "You look but on a stool." Lady Macbeth turned her husband back toward his place at the banquet table.

Macbeth took a few hesitant steps toward his seat. His wife signaled, and a servant brought him a fresh goblet. He raised it. "I drink to the general joy of the whole table. And to our dear friend Banquo, whom we miss. Would that he were here!"

No sooner had he spoken, than Banquo's bloody ghost reappeared. Macbeth flung his goblet through the apparition. "Quit my sight!" he shouted. "Let the earth hide thee!" The ghost vanished. Macbeth sank to his knees.

Lady Macbeth moved between her husband and the nobles. "I pray you, speak not," she told the baffled men. "He grows worse and worse. Please go at once!" The nobles left the banquet hall.

Word of Macbeth's strange behavior quickly spread across

M
A
C
B
E
T
H

Scotland. It fueled the passions of those who suspected that Macbeth was Duncan's murderer.

Macbeth, feeling the threat to his throne, rode back to the barren heath where he and Banquo had first met the witches. He found the three hags stirring a large pot and chanting. "Double, double toil and trouble. Fire burn and cauldron bubble. Eye of newt, and toe of frog, wool of bat, and tongue of dog. Cool it with a baboon's blood. Then the charm is firm and good!"

As the king approached, one witch turned to the others with a leering grin. "By the pricking of my thumbs, something wicked this way comes," the witch said.

Then, before Macbeth could state his business, the witches began a frenzied dance around their cauldron. Wisps of foul greengray mist rose from the simmering liquid. The mists slowly formed a ghostly helmet. The apparition grew and hung over Macbeth. "Beware Macduff!" the faceless helmet warned. "Beware the Thane of Fife." Then it was sucked back into the cauldron.

A second apparition soon appeared, this one in the form of a blood-covered infant. "Laugh to scorn the power of man," the bloody baby moaned. "For none of woman born shall harm Macbeth."

The third apparition was a child. The child wore a crown and held a small tree in his hand. "Macbeth shall never vanquished be, until Great Birnam Wood to high Dunsinane Hill shall come," the child said.

Macbeth rode home mulling over what the witches had

revealed. Their three apparitions, though bizarre, had brought him some peace. Had the witches not as good as proclaimed him invincible? For what man is not born of woman? And how could a forest move to Dunsinane Hill on which his castle stood? As for the Scottish thane Macduff, who had once been his friend, Macbeth would deal with him as he had with Banquo.

Before Macbeth could act, however, messengers brought him news that Macduff had fled to England to join Duncan's son Malcolm. The thane and prince would surely raise a force and march on Macbeth's castle.

Macbeth realized he would have to wait and kill Macduff in battle. But in the meantime, he could make Macduff wish himself dead. Macbeth dispatched murderers to Macduff's castle with the order to kill his entire household: wife, children, and servants all.

"I'll crown my thoughts with acts," Macbeth vowed. But as his resolve grew steely, his once-strong wife unraveled.

By day, Lady Macbeth struggled to appear royal and dignified. But once asleep, guilt drove her from her comfortable bed. The queen walked in her sleep. She wrung her hands as if washing away Duncan's blood. She examined her fingers closely, then scrubbed again. "Out, damned spot!" she cried. "Will these hands never be clean? Here's the smell of blood still." Lady Macbeth walked and rubbed and muttered and wailed until daylight broke, then woke exhausted.

Macbeth himself grew weary as the days passed. The war news

was bad. Malcolm and Macduff's force of ten thousand English soldiers was advancing. The Scottish thanes that had once sat at Macbeth's banquet table were now organizing to join the prince and thane. Malcolm intended to take back the crown he saw as rightfully his. But Macbeth was certain that he had something more powerful than the largest army. He had the witches' prophecies.

"Bring me no more reports; let the false thanes fly all," Macbeth told the messenger who brought news of war. "Till Birnam Wood remove to Dunsinane, I cannot taint with fear."

Prince Malcolm, meanwhile, had met the Scottish thanes at that same Birnam Wood. He was confident about his force, but he knew Macbeth had scouts in the area. Malcolm wanted the advance of his army to remain a deadly surprise. He looked at the trees in Birnam Wood. They were so thick you could not tell where one tree ended and the other began. "Let every soldier hew him down a branch and bear it before him," the prince ordered. "Thereby shall we shadow our numbers." This done, Malcolm's army resumed its march toward Macbeth's castle at Dunsinane.

The castle at Dunsinane was well fortified. Macbeth had raised the drawbridge and bolted the door against his enemies to force them to attempt a dangerous attack. But the fortress felt like a prison.

As he paced up and down inside the castle, Macbeth heard screams. A servant rushed up to him. "The queen, my lord, is dead by her own hand," the shaken servant said.

Macbeth's expression did not change. He had seen too much death already. "She should have died hereafter," he said dully. "Life's but a walking shadow, a poor player that struts and frets his hour upon the stage, and then is heard no more. It is a tale told by an idiot, full of sound and fury, signifying nothing." Macbeth sank down onto his throne.

Then a scout entered, wringing his cap. "Gracious my lord, as I did stand my watch upon the hill, I looked toward Birnam . . . " The scout cleared his throat. "And methought the wood began to move."

Macbeth leaped to his feet. "Liar!" he shouted. But he knew no reason the servant would invent such a tale. Somehow the treacherous witches had tricked him. "Fear not, till Birnam Wood do come to Dunsinane," they had said. Now it seemed Macbeth did have something to fear. But he would not await his fate locked up inside his castle. Macbeth was a warrior. He would meet Malcolm's army on the battlefield.

As the enemy soldiers approached, Macbeth rushed out into the fray. He was soon met by Macduff, whose only desire was to kill this villain who had so brutally slain his family.

Macbeth turned away from his old friend. "Get thee back, my soul is too much charged with blood of thine already."

Macduff drew his weapon. "My voice is in my sword," he replied. "Turn hellhound, turn!"

"Thou losest labor," Macbeth said as they crossed swords. "I

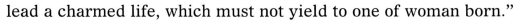

lead a charmed life, which must not yield to one of woman born."

"Despair thy charm," his rival replied. "Macduff was from his mother's womb untimely ripped."

Macbeth's sword suddenly felt as if it weighed a ton. Macduff had had a cesarean birth. In this narrow sense, he was not of woman born. The witches had tricked Macbeth again. Now Macbeth knew he had met his conqueror—but he refused to yield without a fight.

"Before my body, I throw my warlike shield: lay on, Macduff!" Macbeth shouted. He swung his sword with reckless ferocity. Each jab at Macduff was a desperate strike against his own fate. Metal clashed against metal. Blade met flesh. But in the end, Macbeth fell beneath Macduff's avenging sword. The hero who longed to be king, but was crowned a tyrant, was no more.

THE TEMPEST

After being overthrown by his rivals, Prospero, the Duke of Milan and a master magician, ends up on a deserted island. Now a tempest has brought those same enemies to his shores. Prospero faces a difficult dilemma: Should he use his wizardry just to regain his title? Or should he seek sweet revenge?

Illustration by Mark Teague

THE TEMPEST

THE MAIN PLAYERS

PROSPERO, *the deposed Duke of Milan*

MIRANDA, *Prospero's daughter*

ARIEL, *Prospero's spirit servant*

CALIBAN, *Prospero's servant, son of the witch Sycorax*

ANTONIO, *Prospero's brother and the current Duke of Milan*

ALONSO, *King of Naples*

FERDINAND, *Prince of Naples*

SEBASTIAN, *King Alonso's brother*

STEPHANO, TRINCULO, *King Alonso's servants and clowns*

THE TIME & PLACE

16TH CENTURY, AN ISLAND IN THE MEDITERRANEAN SEA

Prince Ferdinand of Naples clung to the

ship's railing. The deck dropped beneath his feet, then just as suddenly thrust him high above the waves. Thunder roared, and balls of fiery lightning lit the masts.

Ferdinand searched the blinding downpour for the rest of the royal party: his father, King Alonso; his uncle Sebastian, Duke Antonio of Milan; and the old counselor, Gonzalo. He found no one. A timber snapped with a loud crack. The vessel was splitting apart and would soon sink, sucking the prince down with it. Ferdinand grabbed the rigging and threw himself into the turbulent sea.

On the shore of a nearby island, a feisty young woman fearfully watched the sinking ship. Miranda worried about its poor passengers—and she wondered about the fierce storm. There was something unnatural about this tempest, something almost magical. She watched the thunderclouds, which seemed to attack the ship like wolves hunting a rabbit.

Miranda ran from the shore. She had never seen a ship before, or indeed, any human other than Prospero, her father. But she had seen plenty of magic. Prospero was a skilled magician who ruled over all the creatures and spirits of the isolated island. Miranda knew her father was a just man, but he took swift action if crossed.

Miranda found her father standing on a high ledge looking out to sea. He watched the storm with satisfaction.

"If by your art, my dearest father, you have put the wild waters in this roar, allay them," Miranda pleaded. "O, I have suffered with those that I saw suffer!"

"Wipe thou thine eyes," Prospero replied calmly. "I have so safely ordered that there is no soul lost. I have done nothing but in care of thee, who art ignorant of what thou art."

Prospero then told his daughter a most amazing story, which revealed their true identities. Miranda was a princess because Prospero himself was the rightful Duke of Milan. He had been overthrown by his own brother, Antonio. King Alonso of Naples and Alonso's brother, Sebastian, had helped.

Antonio had set Prospero and three-year-old Miranda adrift in a leaky open boat. They survived, thanks to a sympathetic counselor, Gonzalo. He had secretly stocked the boat with food and other necessities, including volumes of magic spells from Prospero's library. Father and daughter floated safely to the deserted island, where they had lived for the past twelve years.

"Now," Prospero concluded. "By accident most strange, my enemies have been brought to this shore." Fate had favored Prospero. All his enemies had been aboard the same ship. When it sailed within range of Prospero's power, he unleashed the tempest. This storm was part of the magician's plan to right the wrongs done to him and his daughter.

His story told, Prospero flashed a hand in front of Miranda's eyes. "Thou art inclined to sleep," he said. "Give way to it. I know thou canst not choose."

Miranda yawned. Her eyelids shut and she fell asleep.

Prospero called out, "I am ready now, my Ariel. Hast thou done as I bade thee?"

A nimble little spirit lighted on a mossy rock above Miranda. "To every article," Ariel laughed, lounging on the soft green carpet. "All but the sailors plunged in the foaming brine and quit the vessel. I have dispersed them about the isle. Safely in harbor is the king's ship. The sailors all under hatches stowed, who, with a charm, I have left asleep." The spirit was proud of his work.

"Thy charge exactly is performed," Prospero said. "But there's more work."

"Is there more toil?" Ariel asked crossly. "Let me remember thee what thou hast promised . . . my liberty."

"Before the time be out?" Prospero thundered. "Dost thou forget from what a torment I did free thee? Hast thou forgot the foul witch Sycorax who for sorceries terrible was hither left by sailors?"

At the witch's name, Ariel leaped to his feet. "No, sir!"

"Thou was then her servant," Prospero said sternly. "But because thou wast a spirit too delicate to act her abhorred commands, she did confine thee into a cloven pine tree. Imprisoned thou didst remain a dozen years, within which time she died and left thee there. Thy groans did make wolves howl. It was mine art that opened the pine and let thee out."

THE TEMPEST

"Pardon, master." Ariel bowed respectfully.

Prospero's frown softened. "After two days I will discharge thee," he said.

Ariel clapped his hands in delight. "That's my noble master!" He sped away to carry out Prospero's orders.

With another wave of his hand, Prospero awakened Miranda. He bid her accompany him to visit their servant Caliban, the son of the witch Sycorax.

"What ho! Caliban!" Prospero called into the creature's cave.

"A southwest wind blow on ye and blister you all over!" a rough voice hurled back. Caliban edged his way out into the light. He was of monstrous size. His mass of hair looked like tangled seaweed. He stared at Prospero and Miranda with hatred. "When thou first came, thou stroked me and made much of me; wouldst give me water with berries in it," Caliban said. "And then I loved thee. I showed thee all the qualities of the isle, the fresh springs, brine-pits, barren place and fertile. Cursed be I that did so! For here you keep me in this hard rock, away from the rest of the island."

"I have treated thee with humane care, and lodged thee in mine own cell!" Prospero was so furious, he could scarcely spit out a reply. The creature knew full well that he had been banished because he had tried to attack Miranda.

The memory brought angry tears to Miranda's eyes. "I pitied thee, took pains to make thee speak, taught thee each hour one thing or other," she said.

"You taught me language," Caliban spat, "and my profit on it is, I know how to curse."

Prospero raised his staff. "Fetch us in firewood, and be quick. If thou neglects what I command, I'll rack thee with cramps and make thee roar such that beasts shall tremble at thy din."

"No, pray thee!" Caliban hurried away, muttering. "I must obey, his art is of such power."

On a nearby shore, Prince Ferdinand awoke to find himself lying alone in the sunbaked sand. All signs of the storm—and the ship—had vanished. But his clothes were dry and freshly pressed. Even his sword still hung in its sheath. As Ferdinand wondered at this, Ariel, who remained invisible, began to sing:

> *Full fathom five thy father lies;*
>
> *Of his bones are coral made;*
>
> *Those are the pearls that were his eyes;*
>
> *Nothing of him that doth fade*
>
> *But doth suffer a sea-change*
>
> *Into something rich and strange.*
>
> *Sea nymphs hourly ring his knell:*
>
> *Hark! Now I hear them — Ding-dong bell.*

Ferdinand tried to followed the sound. The spirit's spellbinding melody drew him inland toward Miranda, just as Prospero had commanded.

THE TEMPEST

When they drew near and Miranda saw the prince, she gasped. "What is it? A spirit? I might call him a thing divine. For nothing natural I ever saw so noble."

Ferdinand stared at Miranda, equally amazed. "This is most sure the goddess on whom this music attends!"

Miranda laughed and Ferdinand knew at once she was human. He was delighted to find that Miranda spoke his language, and even knew of his country.

Prospero hid a smile. It was part of the plan for his daughter and his enemy's son to fall in love. And they were doing so without the aid of his magic!

"This swift business I must uneasy make," Prospero said to himself, "lest too light winning make the prize light." The magician lifted his staff against Ferdinand. "Thou hast put thyself upon this island as a spy to win it from me," Prospero charged. "I'll chain thy neck and feet together!"

Startled, the prince drew his sword.

"I can disarm thee with this staff," Prospero warned.

Ferdinand's sword grew heavier and heavier. It fell from his grasp. The prince was too love struck to care. "This man's threats are but light to me, might I but through my prison once a day behold this maid," he said. Miranda begged her father not to treat the prince harshly. Prospero told Ferdinand he would have to prove himself by following all of the magician's commands.

On the other side of the island, King Alonso, along with most of his royal party, had escaped the shipwreck. Still, he despaired because his beloved son, Prince Ferdinand, was missing.

"You have cause of joy, for our escape is much beyond our hope," his counselor, Gonzalo, said gently.

"Sir, Ferdinand may live," another of the king's companions said. "I saw him beat the waves under him and ride upon their backs."

As the royal party rested, Ariel flew above and cast a sleep charm over all but Prospero's brother, Antonio, and King Alonso's brother, Sebastian.

Antonio stared at the sleeping men. An evil thought took hold of him. If Ferdinand had drowned, and if something now happened to King Alonso, then Sebastian would inherit the throne. If Antonio got rid of Alonso, the new king would surely reward him. "My strong imagination sees a crown dropping upon thy head," Antonio whispered to Sebastian.

Sebastian understood immediately. He motioned to Antonio to kill the king while he drew his sword to dispatch the faithful Gonzalo.

Ariel quickly broke the sleeping charm.

"How now?" King Alonso cried, waking to see their swords. "Why are you drawn?"

"We heard a hollow burst of bellowing like bulls," Sebastian stammered, "or rather lions."

THE TEMPEST

The king frowned at the two men. He stood up. "Let's make further search for my poor son," he commanded the party.

Close by, Caliban was gathering firewood in the forest. "All the infections that the sun sucks up from bogs, fens, flats, on Prospero fall, and make him a disease!" he grumbled.

Something shrieked and rustled in the bushes.

"Here comes a spirit of his to torment me for bringing wood in slowly!" Caliban cried. "I'll fall flat. Perchance he will not mind me." He threw a cloth over himself and lay down, shaking with fear.

Another shriek followed. Then suddenly Trinculo, King Alonso's clownish servant, burst forth. He was looking for shelter from the storm. Trinculo spotted the large, covered figure and crept under the cloth with Caliban. "Misery acquaints a man with strange bedfellows," he said.

A voice, loud with drunken song, rang out. Stephano, King Alonso's butler, staggered into the area. He had washed ashore with a case of wine, and had spent the last hour swigging from a bottle. When he saw Caliban's scale-covered skin peeking out from under the cloth, he weaved to a halt. "This is some monster of the isle," Stephano slurred. "If I can recover him, and keep him tame, he's a present for any emperor." The servant smiled as he thought about the royal favors he would surely gain in return.

"Do not torment me, prithee," Caliban cried. "I'll bring my wood home faster."

Stephano eyed the shivering lumpen figure. "He's in a fit now," he concluded. "He shall taste of my bottle." Stephano drained half of its contents into Caliban's mouth. Suddenly, another mouth appeared. Stephano filled that one, too.

"Stephano!" the second mouth cried.

Now the butler knew he had had too much to drink!

The creature divided into two. "It's me, Trinculo. I'm alive!"

Stephano was overjoyed to see his friend and fellow servant.

Meanwhile, Caliban felt the wine work upon his brain and his tongue. Surely, this was a god come to feed him with powerful magic! "Hast thou not dropped from heaven?" he asked Stephano.

Stephano laughed that this green-scaled monster would think *him* a mystical creature. He gave him more wine.

By now, Caliban was drunk, too. He threw down Prospero's bundle of sticks. "A plague upon the tyrant that I serve. I'll bear him no more sticks, but follow thee. By sorcery he got this isle from me. If thy greatness will revenge it on him thou shalt be lord of it, and I'll serve thee. You are my king." Caliban knelt at Stephano's feet.

Stephano considered Caliban's proposal. Be king of an island with his own faithful servant? He'd do it! "Canst thou bring me to this tyrant?" he asked.

"'Tis a custom with him in the afternoon to sleep." Caliban smiled nastily. "There thou mayst brain him, or with a log batter his skull, or paunch him with a stake, or cut his windpipe with a knife.

And then you'll be free to marry his beautiful daughter."

Stephano took another swig from his bottle. "O brave monster! Lead the way!"

Suddenly, the air filled with strange music. Ariel was present. He used the music's charms to lure the three drunkards deeper into the forest—right toward a patch of thorns!

Ferdinand, meanwhile, was hard at work fulfilling Prospero's commands so he might court his daughter. His latest task was to move a towering pile of logs. It was a grueling, pointless job, but Ferdinand would have moved mountains for Miranda's sake.

When she was certain that her father was engrossed in his books, Miranda ran off to meet the prince. She wanted to help him with his task. He wanted only to talk of his feelings.

"I, beyond all limit of what else is in the world, do love, prize, honor you," Ferdinand swore.

"I am your wife, if you will marry me," Miranda said.

Ferdinand smiled.

"My husband then?" the young woman asked.

"Here's my hand," the prince said.

"And mine, with my heart in it," Miranda replied.

The royal party, meanwhile, had entered a forest clearing, just as Prospero had anticipated. He was ready with more torments! With a flash of light, a banquet table appeared. It was piled high with luscious fruits and exotic foods. The hungry men circled the table warily.

Finally, the king announced, "I will stand to, and feed." At once, the banquet disappeared. Ariel hovered in its place, disguised as an avenging bird with a great beak and sharp talons.

The spirit raised his wings and glared at Alonso, Sebastian, and Antonio. "You are three men of sin! You did supplant good Prospero, and expose him and his innocent child unto the sea." Now the sea had exacted revenge, Ariel continued. It had swallowed Alonso's son in payment for Prospero's drowned daughter. There would be further heartbreak and suffering, the spirit warned, unless the royal party atoned for their foul deeds.

With that, Ariel vanished.

Antonio and Sebastian drew their swords and vowed to fight Ariel if he returned. But King Alonso sunk to his knees, repentant.

At that same moment, Alonso's son stood before the man his father had wronged.

Prospero smiled. "All thy vexations were but my trials of thy love, and thou hast wonderfully stood the test." He joined Ferdinand's hand with Miranda's and gave them permission to marry. The magician conjured up some spirits to dance, sing, and entertain them all.

Suddenly, in the midst of the celebration, Prospero remembered what he had asked Ariel to do with Caliban, Stephano, and Trinculo. "Our revels are ended," he said. He swiftly stopped the show and sent the young couple away, then summoned Ariel.

"Where didst thou leave these varlets?" Prospero asked him.

"They followed my music through toothed briars and thorns, which entered their frail shins," Ariel laughed. "I led them on into the filthy pool beyond your cell." At Prospero's command, Ariel produced an array of rich, shining robes and garments. He hung them on a tree outside Prospero's cell. Then the magician and the spirit hid themselves and watched.

Soon, Caliban, all scratched and mucky, entered the area. Stephano and Trinculo, equally muddy, followed.

"This is the mouth of his cell," Caliban whispered loudly. "No noise, and enter. Do that good mischief which may make this island thine own forever, and I, thy Caliban, forever thy foot-licker."

But Stephano and Trinculo had spotted the gaudy garments Ariel had hung. "By this hand, I'll have that gown!" Trinculo cried.

"It's mine! I'm the king!" Stephano replied.

"Let it alone, and do the murder first," Caliban answered. "If Prospero awake, from toe to crown he'll fill our skins with pinches."

Stephano thrust an armload of fur-trimmed finery at Caliban. "Monster, help to bear this away, or I'll turn you out of my kingdom."

Suddenly, the air filled with snarls and howls. A pack of hound-shaped spirits descended on the would-be assassins and chased them back toward the filthy cesspool.

Ariel threw back his dainty head. "Hark, they roar!"

"At this hour all mine enemies lie at my mercy," Prospero said. "How fares the king and his followers?"

Ariel's smile disappeared. "All prisoners, sir, in the lime grove," he replied. "Your charm so strongly works them, that if you now beheld them, your affections would become tender." Ariel paused. "Mine would, sir, were I human."

Prospero was deeply moved by Ariel's speech. Spirits were not naturally given to pity.

"Hast thou, which art but air, a feeling of their afflictions? And shall not I, one of their kind, be kindlier moved than thou art? The rarer action is in virtue, than in vengeance. Go, release them, Ariel."

"I'll fetch them, sir." Ariel vanished.

Prospero stood alone with his staff and book of charms. He thought about all the powerful magic they had wrought. He would not need that kind of power to rule Milan. "I'll break my staff, bury it in the earth, and drown my book," he vowed. Then the magician went into his cell to put on his old official garments.

When Prospero emerged, the royal party stood before him, still blinking and confused. "Behold, sir king, the wronged Duke of Milan," Prospero declared.

Gonzalo embraced his lord. King Alonso seized the opportunity to make amends. "Thy dukedom I do restore," he told Prospero, "and do entreat thou pardon me my wrongs." Alonso humbly knelt.

Prospero bowed in acceptance. Then he turned to Antonio and Sebastian. "Were I so minded, I here could pluck the king's frown upon you, and justify you traitors. At this time I will tell no tales."

Prospero turned back to Alonso. "I pray you look in my cell. My dukedom since you have given me again, I will repay you with as good a thing."

Prospero lifted the curtain that hung before his cell. Inside, Miranda and Ferdinand sat playing chess.

Miranda stood in wonder at the group before her. Her empty island now seemed filled with human faces. "O brave new world that has such people in it!" she cried.

"'Tis new to thee," Prospero sighed.

Ferdinand embraced his father, then presented Miranda as his future queen.

"O, look, sir! Here is more of us!" Gonzalo waved to a group of sailors, whom Ariel had released from sleep.

"Our ship is as tight as when we first put to sea," the first mate reported. They could sail first thing in the morning.

Three filthy figures then stumbled forward, their garments torn to shreds.

"Is this not Stephano, my drunken butler, and Trinculo, my fool?" the king laughed. "But who is this strange beast?"

Caliban moved forward and stood before Prospero, who forgave him for his disloyalty. Caliban pointed to Stephano. "What a thrice-double ass was I to take this drunkard for a god!" he said. Then he trudged back to his cave, vowing not to emerge until the ship had sailed and taken all the humans with it.

THE TEMPEST

Prospero bid the royal party enter his cell to rest and prepare for the journey to Naples. He would accompany them there for the wedding, then sail home to Milan.

When Prospero was alone, Ariel materialized before him.

Prospero bowed to his magical servant. "This was well done, my tricksy spirit. I shall miss thee," he said. Prospero raised his staff to perform his last magical act. "My Ariel, chick, to the elements be free, and fare thou well!"

Ariel was exhilarated. Freedom! He sang out,

Merrily, merrily shall I live now

Under the blossom that hangs on the bough.

Prospero broke his staff and threw it into the sea. "Now my charms are all o'erthrown," he said, "and what strength I have's mine own." And with that, the Duke of Milan turned to join his guests . . . a magician no more.

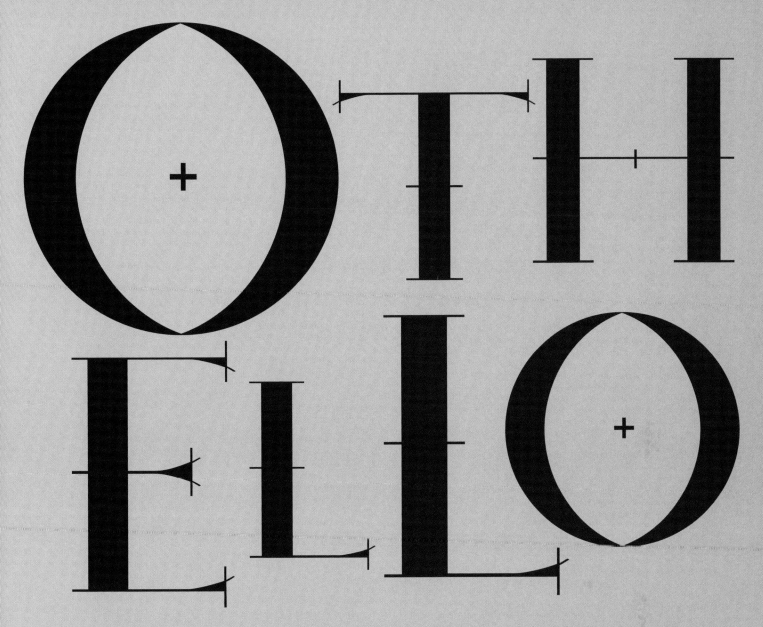

OTHELLO

Othello is about that powerful "green-eyed monster," jealousy. Othello, the general who fears nothing on the battlefield, fears betrayal in the bedroom by his beautiful, courageous wife, Desdemona. Othello's ensign, Iago, is jealous of Cassio, the newly appointed lieutenant who outranks him. Foolish Roderigo jealously wants what he can't have: Desdemona. And behind all the spying, fighting, treachery, and *murder* is the man Othello trusts the most, Iago. "Knavery's plain face is never seen, till us'd." Indeed!

Illustration by Kadir Nelson

OTHELLO

THE MAIN PLAYERS

OTHELLO, *an African prince, who became general of the army of Venice, Italy*

CASSIO, *Othello's lieutenant (second-in-command)*

IAGO, *Othello's ensign (third-in-command)*

BRABANTIO, *a Venetian senator*

DESDEMONA, *Brabantio's daughter*

RODERIGO, *a Venetian gentleman*

EMILIA, *Iago's wife*

THE TIME & PLACE

16TH CENTURY, VENICE, ITALY,
AND CYPRUS, A MEDITERRANEAN ISLAND

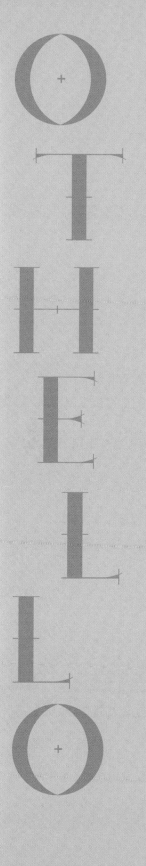

Long ago in Venice, one man stood taller than all

the rest. One man's brave deeds and battle victories thrilled the citizens. One man was the hero of all Venice. . . .

Othello!

Venice loved the fearless, dark-skinned Moor who headed the duke's army. But the Venetian who loved Othello best was Desdemona, Senator Brabantio's daughter. When the general visited her father, Desdemona found excuses to linger. She hung on Othello's every word. Her heart was enflamed by the story of Othello's life: his noble birth in a far-off land, his disastrous capture by an enemy, his hairbreadth escape from slavery, his daring adventures thereafter.

One day, Desdemona finally had a chance to meet Othello alone. She shyly told him that a man need only tell her a story like Othello's and she would fall in love with him. Othello heard what Desdemona's heart was saying and acted swiftly. He asked Desdemona to marry him.

Soon after the two lovers wed in secrecy. They knew that Desdemona's father would oppose the match. Othello may have been the city's greatest hero, but to Senator Brabantio only a Venetian nobleman would make a proper husband for his daughter. A foreigner, especially a Moor from Africa, was unacceptable.

Love called Othello, but so did duty. He was in the midst of choosing a lieutenant, his second-in-command. The choice narrowed

OTHELLO

to two strong candidates: the nobleman Cassio and the soldier Iago. Cassio was a brilliant military strategist, but had little experience on the battlefield. Iago had fought fiercely alongside Othello in many a battle. Nonetheless, Othello chose Cassio. He appointed Iago his ensign, or third-in-command.

Many people in the new ensign's place might only have been disappointed, but Iago was blinded by jealous fury. He vowed to get rid of Cassio and take revenge on Othello. Iago swore he'd weave a web of lies that would ensnare them both. But he would be crafty; Othello and Cassio would never suspect a thing. "Honest Iago," they called him because they thought he was so trustworthy.

Deception was second nature to the wily ensign. For months, Iago had been pretending to help a foolish nobleman named Roderigo court Desdemona. Iago promised to deliver Roderigo's many love notes, gifts, and jewels to her. But the presents never left his own pocket.

When Iago discovered that his general had secretly married Desdemona, he saw his first opportunity to hurt Othello. And he could get lovesick Roderigo to help him.

Iago roused Roderigo in the middle of the night and dragged him to Senator Brabantio's darkened house.

"Awake, what ho, Brabantio! Thieves! Thieves! Thieves!" the two men shouted.

Brabantio stumbled to the window in his bedclothes. Iago, his face hidden by darkness, called up to the senator, "Your daughter hath made a gross revolt . . . you have lost half your soul." Roderigo then told the senator that Desdemona had eloped with Othello.

As Brabantio frantically searched his daughter's bedroom, Iago told Roderigo that Othello was meeting with the duke in the great council chamber of Venice. There was an urgent threat of war, he explaincd, and Othello would soon be sent to fight. Roderigo should bring Brabantio to that chamber, Iago said. Then he slipped away.

Brabantio and Roderigo raced off. They burst into the duke's council, interrupting the discussion of battle plans. The irate senator desperately appealed to the duke for help. "My daughter, O my daughter," Brabantio wailed. "Stolen from me and corrupted by spells." Brabantio was quite certain that his daughter could never have fallen in love with a dark-skinned Moor. Surely, Othcllo must have used some wicked magic charm to woo her.

The duke turned to his mighty general. Othello stepped forward and explained how he had won Desdemona's heart. "She loved me for the dangers I had pass'd," Othello said. "And I loved her that she did pity them. This is the only witchcraft I have used," he swore.

The duke sent for Brabantio's daughter. The beautiful young woman entered and lovingly took Othello's hand. "Here's my husband," Desdemona told her father. "As much duty as my mother showed you, so I show to Othello."

Brabantio was livid! His face flushed red with anger. He glared at Othello. "Look to her, Moor," Brabantio said, "if thou has eyes to see. She has deceived her father, and may thee." The senator stormed off without so much as a backward glance at this daughter.

The duke declared the matter settled. His council returned to discussing the coming war. The duke's enemies, the Turks, were expected to attack the Venetian island of Cyprus. The duke ordered Othello to lead a fleet of ships to stop them.

Desdemona begged to go to Cyprus with Othello; the duke consented. Within the hour, Othello set sail. Cassio was aboard a second ship close by. Iago, Desdemona, and her lady-in-waiting, Emilia, who was Iago's wife, sailed on a third boat at a safe distance behind. Scheming Iago had arranged for Roderigo to sell all his belongings and travel with them. "Thus ever do I make this fool my purse," he laughed to himself.

Othello's warships set course to block the invading Turks. His soldiers were primed for a fight. In the end, it was the sea that won the battle for Venice. The most destructive storm that Cyprus had ever seen scattered the Turks' heavy ships like dead leaves. The badly damaged Turkish fleet turned sail and retreated. In the squall, Cassio lost sight of Othello's ship. When the lieutenant reached Cyprus, he was anxious for news of his friend and commander.

Iago's ship docked next. Cassio was happy to see his friend

Desdemona, though he could give the anxious bride no certain news of her husband.

As Cassio spoke warmly to Desdemona, a sly smile spread across Iago's face. His first attempt at revenge had failed. But now a sweeter idea presented itself. Iago would convince Othello that Desdemona was having an affair with Cassio. He privately sneered at the handsome nobleman's courtly manners—a kiss here, a bow there. "He takes her by the palm," Iago chuckled. "Ay, smile upon her, do! With as little a web as this will I ensnare as great a fly as Cassio."

A cry shook Iago out of his jealous daydream. A ship's mast appeared on the horizon. Everyone rushed to the water's edge. Othello's ship soon sailed safely into port. Desdemona ran forward to meet her husband. Othello kissed her forehead. "If after every tempest comes such contentment, may the winds blow till they have wakened death!" he murmured.

Since the Turkish invasion was no longer a threat, Othello ordered a night of feasting and celebration throughout Cyprus. The general was eager to spend time with his new bride. Othello charged Cassio with keeping the watch. As ever, Iago kept watch, too.

The evil ensign soon found Roderigo and pulled him aside. "Desdemona is in love with Cassio," Iago whispered. "After all, it's only natural that she tire of the ugly Moor. Cassio is young and handsome and has all the advantages a young Venetian woman

O
T
H
E
L
L
O

desires." Iago convinced the foolish Roderigo that if they could just get rid of Cassio, Desdemona would be his at last.

That evening, Iago put his plan into action. He found Cassio on duty and bullied him into drinking a toast to the general's health—and then another, and another. By the time he returned to his post, Cassio was drunk.

Goaded on by Iago, Roderigo then picked a fight with the befuddled Cassio. The lieutenant rose to the bait. Cassio grew loud, belligerent, and threatening. The governor of Cyprus stepped in to stop the matter. The drunken Cassio wounded him. At Iago's urging, Roderigo ran through the streets yelling, "Riot! Riot!" The whole town was thrown into a panic.

Othello rushed to the scene. Furious at Cassio for destroying the peace he was charged to protect, the general dismissed him. "Cassio, I love thee; but never more be officer of mine," Othello said. He turned his back on his friend and strode off.

Cassio stood lost and alone. He was devastated at being discharged. "My reputation, my reputation," he moaned, "I have lost my reputation."

Iago sidled up to his rival. He spoke to Cassio as if he were a concerned friend. "Ask Desdemona's help to put you again in her husband's good graces," Iago urged. "She is so kind that she'll do whatever you ask and more." Cassio sped away to seek out Desdemona. Iago laughed. "I'll pour this poison in Othello's ear—

that his wife wants Cassio reinstated because she desires him. Then however much she strives to help Cassio, that much she'll hurt her own reputation with her husband."

When he reached the castle, Cassio begged for an audience with Desdemona. As Iago had predicted, the sweet-tempered young woman easily agreed to plead her friend's case. "My husband shall never rest until this matter is resolved," she assured him. "His home shall seem a school, with every lesson about Cassio's loyal service."

Meanwhile, Iago intentionally guided Othello to the garden where Desdemona and Cassio spoke. As they approached, Cassio grew nervous.

"I'm not fit to speak to the general right now. I'm too ashamed," he told Desdemona. "I'll take my leave."

Iago watched Cassio slink off and scowled disapprovingly. "Ha! I like not that," he muttered.

Othello looked warily at his ensign. "Was that not Cassio parted from my wife?" he asked.

"Surely not," Iago said slyly. "Cassio wouldn't steal away, so guilty-like, seeing you coming."

Othello frowned. He had learned to trust Iago's instincts on the battlefield. That certainly was Cassio. Did Iago have reason to suspect him . . . with Desdemona? Othello eyed his wife uncertainly. But when Desdemona approached, she took his rough hands and brought them

OTHELLO

to her tender lips. All Othello's doubts melted away. He kissed her.

Her lips pressed his for a moment, then she stepped back. "I've just spoken to Cassio, my lord," Desdemona said. "If I have any power to move you, call him back. Reinstate him, he is sorry for what he has done." She heaped praise upon Cassio and pushed Othello to name the exact hour he would see his ex-lieutenant.

Desdemona's urgent pleas grated on Othello. "I will deny thee nothing," he told her, "but leave me be for now." Desdemona curtsied slightly and departed.

Othello turned to Iago. "When Cassio left my wife, why did you say 'I like not that'?"

Iago was far too shrewd to directly accuse Cassio and Desdemona. Othello's first instinct would be to defend his wife—perhaps with drawn sword. Instead Iago said, "It were not for your quiet nor your good to let you know my thoughts."

Othello commanded Iago to speak. "Think'st thou that I would make a life of jealousy? I assure you that I'll see proof before I doubt my wife's faithfulness."

"Now I can speak freely," Iago said. He claimed that one night, as he bunked next to Cassio in the officer's lodgings, he overheard the lieutenant talking in his sleep. "I heard Cassio say, 'Sweet Desdemona, let us be wary, let us hide our loves!'" Iago reported. "And then he laid his leg over my thigh and kissed me hard, as if he plucked up kisses by the roots."

Had Cassio been reliving a secret meeting with Desdemona? The thought of another man kissing his wife filled Othello with anger. "Monstrous! Monstrous!" he cried.

Iago looked concerned. "It's just that I would not have your noble nature abused," he told Othello. "The women of Venice are skilled in deceiving their husbands—much as Desdemona deceived her father in marrying you." Noting the general's changed expression, he added, "I see this has a little dashed your spirits."

"Not a jot," Othello insisted and sent Iago away. But in truth jealousy gnawed at his soul. Now he could not think of Desdemona without imagining her in Cassio's arms—or in his bed. "Oh, curse of marriage," he groaned, "that we can call these delicate creatures ours, but not their appetites!"

By the time Desdemona and Emilia came to fetch him for dinner, Othello's head was throbbing. His wife offered to bind his forehead with her handkerchief to ease the pain. But he pushed the cloth away and it drifted to the ground unnoticed.

Emilia dropped behind the pair and scooped up the handkerchief. She saw it was the special handkerchief that Othello's mother had given to him and he had given to his wife. Emilia's husband, Iago, had often pressured her to steal it. Emilia had refused. But here she had found the handkerchief on the ground. Why shouldn't she borrow it and have the design copied for her husband?

When Iago saw the handkerchief, he snatched it from Emilia

and shooed his wife away. Now he had the proof he needed!

"I will lose this in Cassio's lodgings," Iago laughed to himself. "Perhaps Othello will see him with it. And in any case Desdemona will not be able to produce it if he asks. Trifles light as air are to jealous minds confirmations strong as proofs of holy writ."

Othello approached, moaning and muttering to himself. Gone was his soldier's strutting step. Now he staggered like a madman. His thoughts tormented him.

When Othello saw Iago, he grabbed him by the collar and hauled him to his feet. "Villain, be sure thou prove my love a whore! Give me visible proof!"

Iago eased himself out of the general's powerful grip. "Have you not sometimes seen a handkerchief spotted with strawberries in your wife's hand?" he asked.

"'Twas my first gift to her," Othello said hoarsely. The handkerchief had been his mother's most treasured possession. She swore it had magic charms that protected a couple's love.

"Such a handkerchief did I today see Cassio wipe his beard with," Iago lied.

Othello's features twisted in fury. The thought of this precious token in another man's hand was more than he could bear. "All my fond love thus do I blow to heaven," he raged. "'Tis gone. Arise, black vengeance, from that hollow hell." His heart pounded. "Oh, blood, blood, blood!" he cried. Othello turned to Iago with gritted teeth.

"Within three days let me hear you say that Cassio's not alive."

Iago nodded. Now his revenge against Cassio was sealed. But he had more poisoned words for Othello. "My friend Cassio is as good as dead," he said. Then he added slyly, "But let Desdemona live."

Othello's eyes blazed with rage. "No, damn her, lewd minx."

Iago knelt before Othello. "I here give my wit, hands, heart to wronged Othello's service. Let him command what bloody business ever," he said.

Othello embraced him. "Now art thou my lieutenant," he told Iago. "I am your own forever," Iago answered.

A trumpet's flourish filled the air, and Desdemona escorted in a delegation from Venice. They bore new orders from the duke. Since the Turkish fleet was no more, Othello was called back to Venice. The duke's force in Cyprus would be led by Cassio, whom the duke still imagined to be Othello's lieutenant.

Othello overheard Desdemona warning one of the delegates, her cousin, that Cassio had Othello's ill favor. When his wife began to take Cassio's side, Othello grew livid. He slapped Desdemona and ordered her from his sight. The Venetian delegates were confounded. Could this be the noble Othello whom the duke trusted so completely?

Taking his leave of the visitors, Othello cornered Desdemona. He demanded that she show him his mother's handkerchief. Afraid to admit the keepsake was missing, Desdemona insisted it was tucked away safely.

"Heaven truly knows that thou art false as hell," Othello snarled. "Oh, thou weed, who art so lovely fair that the senses ache at thee, would thou had'st ne'er been born!" He ordered Desdemona to wait for him in their bedchamber and to dismiss her maid once she was ready for bed. Then he stormed off.

Desdemona was frightened and bewildered. There must be some mistake. What had she done to deserve her husband's displeasure? Determined to make amends, she and her maid, Emilia, obediently went up to the bedchamber. Emilia was worried and tried to talk to Desdemona, but her lady sent her away.

Meanwhile, outside the castle walls, Iago plotted Cassio's murder. First, he convinced the gullible Roderigo that killing Cassio was the only way for him to win Desdemona. Then, Iago led Roderigo to a dark alley near where Cassio was dining that night. A short time later, Cassio passed by. Roderigo leaped from the shadows and jabbed a knife blade in Cassio's chest.

But the lieutenant wore a thick coat.

Cassio, unhurt, spun around, drew his sword and stabbed his attacker. As Cassio stood there dazed, Iago darted by and viciously slashed his leg. Cassio crumpled to the ground, crying for help. "Murder! Murder!"

Iago heroically charged in. He pretended to comfort Cassio and vowed to avenge the lieutenant. He crossed over to the wounded

Roderigo and drove a knife into his heart. There was no danger now of Roderigo ever revealing Iago's role in this wicked plot.

Othello heard the cries and believed Cassio was dead. Now all that remained was to bring Desdemona to justice, he thought. Othello slowly entered the bedchamber and bent over his wife's sleeping form. She looked so beautiful. He could not resist giving her one last kiss . . . and then another . . . and then another.

Othello's kisses awakened Desdemona. "Have you prayed tonight?" he asked her. "I would not kill thy soul."

Kill? Desdemona was frantic. She tried to reason with Othello, "I never did offend you in my life," Desdemona swore. She begged for mercy. "O, banish me, my lord, but kill me not!" Her pleas fell on deaf ears. With the cool certainty of an executioner, Othello pressed a cushion over his wife's face, smothering her.

Emilia burst in with news about the wounding of Cassio. Seeing Desdemona sprawled across the sheets, she dropped to her knees. "Sweet mistress, speak!"

"'Twas I that killed her," Othello said darkly. "My actions were just. Ask thy husband else. She was false to wedlock with Cassio."

Emilia's screams echoed down the castle halls. "The Moor has kill'd my mistress. Murder, murder, murder!"

The governor and the Venetian noblemen crowded into the bedchamber. Iago rushed to the bedside and Emilia faced him squarely. "Did you ever tell Othello Desdemona was false?"

OTHELLO

"I did," Iago replied.

"You told a lie, an odious lie!" Emilia cried.

Othello scowled. "But she bestowed on Cassio a token of love which I first gave to her. It was an antique handkerchief that once belonged to my mother."

"Oh, thou dull Moor," Emilia said. "That handkerchief I found and did give my husband, for often he begged me to steal it."

The blood drained from Othello's face. At last he saw "honest" Iago's full treachery. "Villain!" he shouted and drew his sword. Othello charged at Iago; the governor stepped between them and wrestled the weapon away. All was chaos. Iago took advantage of the confusion. He rushed forward, stabbed Emilia for telling the truth, then fled down the corridor. The governor's men raced after him.

Othello stumbled to Desdemona's side. "I am one that loved not wisely, but too well," he moaned. "One who threw a pearl away richer than all his tribe." Othello drew a hidden knife from his tunic and plunged it into his own chest. Falling across Desdemona's body, he wept, "I kiss'd thee ere I kill'd thee. No way but this, killing myself to die upon a kiss."

So it was that mighty Othello, hero to many, hated by one, brave in battle but suspicious in love, was brought to ruin by his own jealousy.

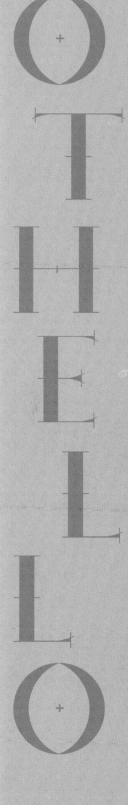

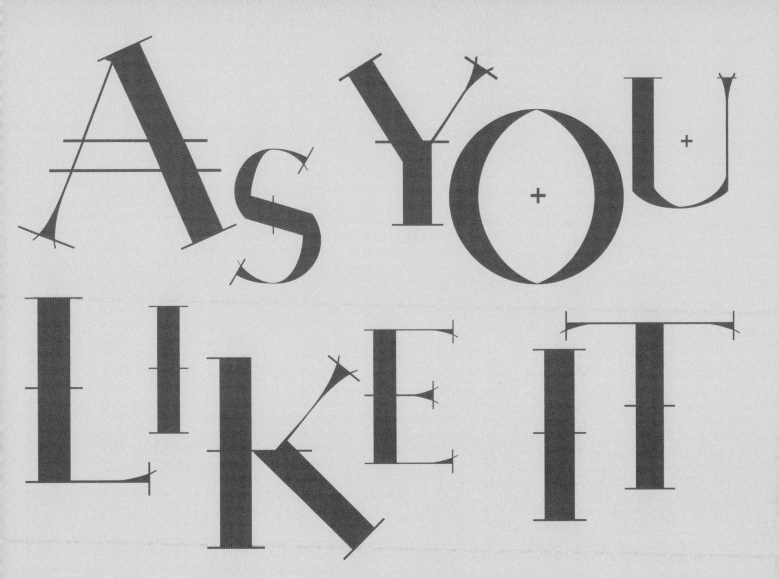

As You Like It

A deposed duke now presides over a woodland court in the Forest of Arden. Meanwhile, the duke's evil brother rules in the royal court. Rosalind and Celia, two young noblewomen, flee to the forest to escape his wrath. So does a young nobleman, Orlando, who hides from his evil older brother within these woods. There, he unwittingly woos his own true love, Rosalind. Dressed as a shepherd boy, she merrily tests the depths of Orlando's passion. In *As You Like It*, heroes, heroines, and knaves all tread the same path—into the woods!

Illustration by Barbara McClintock

AS YOU LIKE IT

THE MAIN PLAYERS

DUKE SENIOR, *rightful ruler of the kingdom, now in exile*

ROSALIND, *Duke Senior's daughter*

FREDERICK, *Duke Senior's younger brother, usurper of the throne*

CELIA, *Frederick's daughter and Rosalind's cousin*

ORLANDO, *a young nobleman*

OLIVER, *Orlando's older brother*

THE TIME & PLACE

A LONG TIME AGO, EUROPE

Long ago in Europe, two royal brothers ruled:

one, over a kingdom in the forest, the other, over a kingdom won through treachery and deceit. Duke Senior, as he was called, was the rightful ruler. But Frederick, his younger brother, stole the throne and banished his elder brother. The duke and many of his loyal followers lived in exile in the Forest of Arden. Frederick ruled mercilessly, but uneasily, at court.

The daughters of these two men, however, loved each other as sisters. Frederick allowed Rosalind, Duke Senior's child, to remain at court for the sake of his own daughter, Celia. The two girls were inseparable.

"What my father hath taken away from thy father, I will render thee in affection," Celia promised Rosalind.

"I will forget the condition of my estate, to rejoice in yours," Rosalind answered.

One day, to amuse themselves, the two girls strolled over to a wrestling contest on the palace grounds. When they reached the field, Frederick called to them. He pointed out a slender young man who had come to court to win money by fighting the court's barrel-chested wrestling champion. Frederick did not relish such an uneven match. "Speak to him, ladies," he urged. "See if you can move him."

Celia approached the stranger. "We pray you for your own sake give over this attempt," she said gently.

AS YOU LIKE IT

AS YOU LIKE IT

"We will make it our suit that the wrestling might not go forward," Rosalind offered.

The young man shook his head. "If I be killed, I shall do my friends no wrong, for I have none to lament me," he said. "Only in the world I fill up a place, which may be better supplied when I have made it empty."

The youth's melancholy reminded Rosalind of her own. At least he was taking bold action, however foolhardy, she thought. Rosalind smiled encouragingly. "The little strength that I have, I would it were with you," she said.

The young man returned her smile, then joined the champion in the ring. Laughing, the burly court wrestler reached out to pat the young man's head. With a quick motion, the challenger twisted the champion's arm behind his back, forcing his face toward the ground.

The court wrestler broke away, his smirk replaced with a scowl. He lunged at the challenger, who ducked, spun, and then yanked his opponent's leg out from under him. The wrestler landed on his back with a dull thud. He did not get up.

Frederick turned from his defeated champion to the young challenger. "Thou art a gallant youth. What is thy name?"

"Orlando, my liege, the youngest son of the late Sir Rowland de Boys."

Frederick's eyes narrowed. "I would thou hadst been son to

some man else. The world esteemed thy father honorable, but I did find him always mine enemy." He stormed back into the palace.

Rosalind studied Orlando's face. "My father loved Sir Rowland as his soul," she whispered to Celia. Rosalind removed a chain from her neck and handed it to Orlando. "Sir, you have wrestled well, and overthrown more than your enemies." Her accidental confession—that Orlando had conquered her heart—brought a flush to her cheeks. She hurried away, with an amused Celia trailing behind.

Orlando was dumbstruck. "What passion hangs these weights upon my tongue? I cannot speak to her." He watched Rosalind until she was out of sight. "O poor Orlando, thou art overthrown!" he said to himself.

A courtier hurried up to the young man. "Leave this place," he whispered to Orlando. "Such is now the duke's bad humor that he misconstrues all you have done," the courtier warned. Orlando agreed to go, but not before the court attendant told him about the two gracious young ladies he had just met.

As Orlando walked home, he thought longingly of Rosalind. Could she love him, despite his unlucky circumstances? Orlando's father was dead and all the family property now belonged to his oldest brother, Oliver. Oliver was supposed to see that Orlando got a gentleman's education, but he was jealous of Orlando's good looks and fine spirit. Oliver kept his younger brother working in the fields, dressed like a laborer and treated like a servant. Now that Orlando

AS YOU LIKE IT

A
S
Y
O
U
L
I
K
E
I
T

was grown, he intended to seek his own fortune. The wrestling match had been his first attempt. If he was going to be a worthy husband for Rosalind, he needed success now more than ever!

Orlando soon reached home. Adam, an old family servant, stopped him from entering.

"Your brother this night means to burn the lodging where you lie and you within it!" the servant warned. He told Orlando that Oliver was in a jealous rage over his brother's wrestling triumph. Adam himself did not want to stay with such a cruel master. The old servant and the youth fled to the nearby Forest of Arden.

Back at the palace, Rosalind was also the target of a jealous rage. Frederick was angry at the sympathy and pity she received from his subjects—especially as more and more of them left to join her father in the forest.

"Get you from our court," Frederick commanded his niece. "If thou be found within twenty miles of here, thou diest for it."

Rosalind was shocked at her sudden banishment. Celia was outraged.

"I cannot live out of her company," she told her father. Both girls then secretly packed their fine dresses and jewels. Celia also took a quantity of gold. They planned to seek out the rightful duke in the Forest of Arden.

The cousins prepared disguises appropriate for country life. Celia dressed as a shepherdess and called herself Aliena. Thinking they would be safer if one of them appeared to be a boy, Rosalind donned male clothing and posed as Ganymede, Aliena's brother. Under cover of night, they stole out of the palace.

When dawn broke, Celia and Rosalind were deep within Arden Forest. They were enchanted by its woodland beauty. They were also hungry and exhausted. Fortunately, they stumbled upon a shepherd with a cottage for sale. Celia gave him the gold she had carried from the palace. Then the cousins set up housekeeping in the little house in the woods.

Orlando and Adam had also traveled all night. They reached another part of the forest. The old man was faint with hunger. He could go no farther. Orlando, pledging to return with food for the faithful servant, set off.

His search brought him to the forest court of Duke Senior. Since his brother had deposed him, Rosalind's father had lived in Arden with a band of loyal lords. They wore rough woodsmen's clothing and hunted their own food. Yet they lived a noble life in the wilderness, learning life's lessons from nature. This day, as the duke and his men sat down to their luncheon banquet, Orlando burst upon them, sword drawn. "He dies that touches any of this fruit till I and my affairs are answered!" he cried.

"As you will not be answered with reason, I must die," answered Jacques, a witty, cynical lord of the duke's court.

Duke Senior offered a plate of grapes to the wild-eyed young

AS YOU LIKE IT

man. "What would you have?" he asked. "Your gentleness shall force more than your force move us to gentleness."

Embarrassed, Orlando lowered his sword. "Pardon me, I pray you. I thought that all things had been savage here." When he explained his situation, the duke told him to fetch Adam to the feast.

The duke recognized at once that Orlando was a gentleman out of favor with fortune. "Thou seest we are not all alone unhappy," he told his lords as they waited for the two travelers to return. "This wide and universal theater presents more woeful pageants than the scene wherein we play in."

The duke's men agreed. "All the world's a stage, and all the men and women merely players," said Jacques. "They have their exits and their entrances, and one man in his time plays many parts."

Orlando returned, carrying Adam on his back. The duke was delighted to discover that Orlando was the son of his old friend Sir Rowland. The two men spent a pleasant meal exchanging compliments and stories. Meanwhile, their brothers had a far less cordial meeting.

Frederick was enraged when he found out that his daughter was gone. He was desperate to find Celia. A maid had overheard the cousins talking with Orlando after the fight. Frederick suspected that the young man had helped the girls escape. He summoned Oliver and demanded to know the whereabouts of his brother

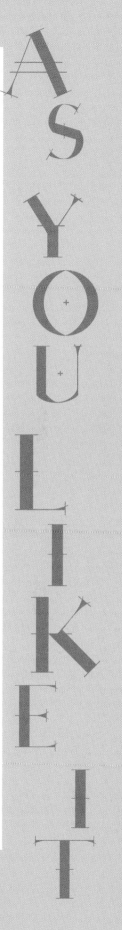

Orlando. Oliver swore he hadn't seen his younger sibling since the wrestling match. Frederick was unmoved. He seized Oliver's property and banished him until he brought Orlando to the palace. After making inquiries about Orlando, Oliver headed toward the Forest of Arden.

Meanwhile, Orlando quickly adjusted to life in the duke's rugged but noble woodland court. Still, he would have traded all his pleasant hours there for five minutes in Rosalind's company. Whenever Orlando was alone, he pressed Rosalind's necklace to his lips. As his yearning grew, it flowered into poems.

Orlando wrote line upon line of heartfelt rhyme—unschooled but full of passion. He nailed these poems to tree trunks for miles around. "Hang there, my verse, in witness of my love," he said. He carved his true love's name on other trunks. "O Rosalind!" he sighed. "These trees shall be my books, and in their barks my thoughts I'll inscribe." How wonderful it would be, Orlando thought, if one of these poems could magically find its way to Rosalind.

Magic, indeed!

In another part of the forest, Rosalind, dressed in boy's clothing, was plucking one of Orlando's poems from a tree trunk.

"Let no face be kept in mind," she read, "but the fair of Rosalind."

Celia approached and dangled another poem before Rosalind's

nose. "Dost thou not wonder how thy name should be hanged and carved upon these trees?" she asked. "It is young Orlando, that tripped up the wrestler's heels and your heart both in an instant."

"Orlando?" Rosalind looked down in horror at her male clothing. "Alas! What shall I do with my doublet and hose?"

Just then, Orlando passed near with Jacques. The two were discussing love, which Jacques dismissed. "The worse fault you have is to be in love," the melancholy lord declared. Rosalind and Celia scrambled to hide behind a tree.

Orlando was as handsome as Rosalind remembered. Even now he was praising her to his companion. Still, Rosalind couldn't help but wonder whether Orlando's love was true. He did write wonderful love poems, but then again they hardly knew each other. Would he even recognize her if he saw her under these changed circumstances? And how could Rosalind find out how deeply she loved Orlando?

Rosalind laughed at the plan that sprung to mind. "I will speak to him like a saucy lackey," she whispered to Celia, "and under that habit play the knave with him." She would get to know Orlando better and test the sincerity of his devotion. Straightening her doublet, Rosalind stepped out from behind the tree.

"Do you hear, forester?" she called, deepening her voice.

Orlando, having just parted company with the lord, turned around to see a fine-featured lad beckoning him.

"There is a man haunts the forest that abuses our young plants with carving 'Rosalind' on their barks," Rosalind said. "If I could meet that fancy-monger, I would give him some good counsel, for he seems to have the fever of love upon him."

"I am he that is so love-shaked," Orlando admitted. "I pray you tell me your remedy. Did you ever cure any so?"

"Yes, one, and in this manner," Rosalind said. "He was to imagine me his love. I would now like him, then loathe him; now entertain him, then forswear him; now weep for him, then spit at him. Thus would I cure you, too, if you would but call me Rosalind and come every day to woo me."

Orlando considered this strange proposal. He did not wish to be cured of his love for Rosalind, but this would give him a chance to practice wooing her. Besides, this boy seemed like jolly company, and everyone else in the duke's court was tired of hearing about his beloved. And in some strange way, the boy even looked like fair Rosalind. Orlando smiled. "Now, by the faith of my love, I will, good youth."

The impish maiden in boy's clothing laughed. "Nay, you must call me Rosalind," she said.

For the next few days, Rosalind enjoyed pretending to be Ganymede pretending to be Rosalind. It gave her license to say and ask many things that a proper young lady never could.

The more Rosalind came to know Orlando, the more she liked

him. He had only one fault that irked her. Orlando was never on time for their meetings. If he could not honor these little commitments, could she count on him to honor a marriage?

Still, whenever he at last arrived, Rosalind found it hard to stay angry. She eagerly fell into their role-playing. "Am I not your Rosalind?" she asked.

Orlando laughed. "I take some joy to say you are, because I would be talking of her."

Rosalind crossed her arms. "Well, in her person, I say I will not have you."

"I would not have my real Rosalind of this mind," Orlando cried. "For I protest her frown might kill me!"

Rosalind laughed at Orlando's melodramatic response. "Men have died from time to time, and worms have eaten them," she said, "but not for love."

At this, Orlando clapped his hat on his head and bowed. "I must attend the duke at dinner. By two o'clock I will be with thee again."

Rosalind frowned. "If you come one minute behind your hour, I will think you the most pathetical break-promise, and the most hollow lover. Therefore, keep your promise."

"With no less religion than if thou were indeed my Rosalind," Orlando swore.

Orlando disappeared into the woods; Rosalind sighed. Two hours later, Celia found Rosalind still sighing in that same spot.

"Is it not past two o'clock?" Rosalind asked glumly.

Celia put a finger to her lips and pointed. Across the brook, a shepherd named Silvius pursued a young shepherdess.

"Sweet Phebe, do not scorn me!" Silvius cried. He flung himself at her feet.

Phebe placed her boot on Silvius's shoulder and toppled him. "Come thou not near me!" Phebe loved to torment Silvius.

Rosalind spoke up. "Foolish shepherd, wherefore do you follow her? You are a thousand times a properer man than she a woman."

Startled, Silvius scrambled to his feet and backed away. But Phebe stood her ground. She smiled flirtatiously. "Sweet youth, I had rather hear you chide than this man woo."

"I pray you do not fall in love with me," Rosalind laughed. "For I am falser than vows made in wine." She quickly led Celia toward their cottage.

On the way, they encountered a stranger dressed in ragged, dirty clothing. He asked if they were the occupants of the shepherd cottage, then bowed and said, "Orlando doth commend him to you both."

The stranger introduced himself as Oliver, Orlando's older brother. Rosalind and Celia were amazed by his harrowing story. Oliver had been sleeping beneath a tree in the forest. A giant snake had coiled around his throat, ready to strike. By good fortune, Orlando came along. The snake slithered off, but a hungry lioness in the bush now seized her chance. The big cat was set to pounce on Oliver. Orlando threw himself between them. The lioness was repulsed, but not before she mauled Orlando's forearm. Astonished by his brother's selfless act, Oliver was profoundly changed. He apologized for all the wrong he had done his brother in the past and swore to do right by him. Orlando was now resting at the duke's forest court.

"He sent me hither," Oliver concluded, "that you might excuse his broken promise. He had sworn to be on time. He asked me to give this napkin, dyed in his blood, unto the shepherd youth that he in sport doth call his Rosalind."

At the sight of Orlando's blood, Rosalind fainted. When she came to, she pretended it was part of her act. Oliver insisted on helping the pair back to their cottage.

As quickly as Orlando and Rosalind had fallen in love, so too did Oliver and Celia. Within hours they had agreed to marry. Oliver rushed back to Orlando to tell him he could have their father's estate. Oliver planned to stay in the woods with his shepherdess love.

Orlando couldn't help feeling a little envious of Oliver's engagement. "O, how bitter a thing it is to look into happiness through another man's eyes!" he confided to Rosalind at their next meeting.

Rosalind looked at Orlando tenderly. He had proven himself both brave and true, she decided. "If you do love Rosalind so near the heart as your gesture cries it out," she said, "when your brother marries Aliena shall you marry her." She promised to produce Rosalind as if by magic.

Before Orlando could question her further, Phebe approached with Silvius trailing behind. Phebe planted herself in front of Rosalind. "Youth, you have done me much ungentleness," she said petulantly.

"Pray you, no more of this," Rosalind laughed. "I will marry you if ever I marry woman, and I'll be married tomorrow. But if you do refuse to marry me, will you give yourself over to this faithful shepherd?"

Phebe nodded impatiently, while Silvius looked confused.

Rosalind told them to meet her at Oliver and Aliena's wedding the following morning at the duke's forest court.

At dawn, Rosalind and Cclia packed away their rough country clothes and dressed in their silken palace gowns. They hung jewelry in each other's hair and slid their feet into ladies' slippers. Then, arm in arm, they set off for the Duke Senior's court.

When Orlando saw Rosalind, he was mystified at first. What was happening here? It suddenly became clear.

"If there be truth in sight, you are my Rosalind!" Orlando cried. He was not angry at being deceived. Instead, he realized that Ganymede had indeed cured him of lovesickness—by giving him the very medicine he craved.

AS YOU LIKE IT

Phebe gaped at Rosalind's transformation from Ganymede. "If sight and shape be true, why then, my love adieu!" She looked up at Silvius with new eyes. This was the man she would marry.

"O my dear niece, welcome thou art to me! Even daughter, welcome, in no less degree." Duke Senior warmly greeted his long-lost daughter and niece. He then called all three couples forward and married them.

As the lovers kissed, a messenger approached with surprising news. Frederick, too, was now in the Forest of Arden. He had been bent on killing his brother, but along the way had met a wise old holy man. The holy man had converted Frederick to a life of monkish solitude. Frederick then restored the kingdom to the rule of his elder brother the duke.

Duke Senior turned to his joyous court. "Everyone of this happy number shall share the good of our returned fortune. Meantime, play, music, and you brides and bridegrooms all, with scales o'er-heaped in joy, to the measures fall." Celia and Rosalind smiled and reached for each other's hands. All had been set right and it was as they liked it.

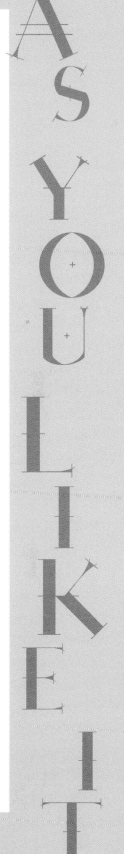

ROMEO AND JULIET

Romeo and Juliet love each other. Their families loathe each other. The star-crossed lovers refuse to let crossed swords part them. But "violent delights have violent ends" in this tragic story of young hearts and ancient quarrels.

Illustration by David Shannon

ROMEO AND JULIET

THE MAIN PLAYERS

LORD & LADY MONTAGUE, *heads of the House of Montague*

ROMEO MONTAGUE

MERCUTIO, BENVOLIO, *Romeo's friends*

LORD & LADY CAPULET, *heads of the House of Capulet*

JULIET CAPULET

NURSE, *the woman who looks after Juliet*

TYBALT, *Juliet's cousin*

THE PRINCE OF VERONA

COUNT PARIS, *the prince's relative and Juliet's suitor*

FRIAR LAURENCE

THE TIME & PLACE

16TH CENTURY, VERONA, ITALY

"What, ho! you men, you beasts. From those bloody hands throw your mistempered weapons to the ground!" the prince of Verona commanded. The Montagues and the Capulets had been fighting . . . again! These two prominent families of Verona nurtured an ancient grudge. Neither the Montagues nor the Capulets remembered what insult or injury sowed the seeds of their hatred. But its roots sank so deep and its canopy spread so wide that the whole city too often tasted the bitter fruit of their brawls.

After this latest bloody fight between the two houses, the prince called the head of each family to account. "If ever you disturb our streets again," he warned Lord Capulet and Lord Montague, "your lives shall pay the forfeit of the peace."

On that summer morning, there was one Montague who was filled not with wretched hate, but with wretched love. Romeo, Lord Montague's only son, pined for beautiful Rosaline, who did not return his affection. His friends, Benvolio and Mercutio, had a plan to help Romeo forget her. The Capulets were giving a magnificent masked ball, where Romeo could meet other beautiful young women. Naturally, no Montagues were invited to this ball, but Benvolio and Mercutio insisted they attend the party anyway. No one would recognize them behind their masks. "Comparc Rosaline's face with some that I shall show," Benvolio assured Romeo, "and I will make thee think thy swan a crow."

ROMEO AND JULIET

ROMEO AND JULIET

Lord Capulet's daughter, Juliet, was also being urged to look for love's face that night. Though she was not yet fourteen, a handsome young nobleman, Count Paris, had asked for permission to marry her. Juliet had never met the gentleman, but her mother assured her she would like what she saw that night. "Read over the volume of young Paris' face," Lady Capulet said. "You'll find delight written there with beauty's pen."

When Romeo and his masked friends arrived at the ball, Romeo planted himself beside a stone pillar. Mercutio and Benvolio eagerly joined the dance. Even with a mask covering part of his face, Romeo was quickly recognized by Lord Capulet's nephew, Tybalt. The hotheaded young man sent his servant for a sword and rushed to tell his uncle that an enemy had crashed the party.

Lord Capulet was in a jovial mood and did not want his fun spoiled. "Young Romeo, is it?" he said. "Nay, let him."

Tybalt argued with his uncle, but Lord Capulet was firm. Tybalt privately swore to make Romeo pay for this intrusion.

Romeo watched the dancing couples, hoping for a glimpse of Rosaline. The dancers wheeled around, spinning Paris's partner into view. The instant Romeo saw Juliet, his heart soared like a dove released from a cage. "Did my heart love till now?" he whispered. He forgot all about Rosaline. "What lady's that, which doth enrich the hand of yonder knight?" he asked a servant. "O, she doth teach the torches to burn bright!" Romeo moved closer.

Juliet, meanwhile, stifled a yawn. True, Paris was handsome and polite, but there was no spark behind his pale blue eyes. As they danced, Juliet wondered what it felt like to be truly in love. Her suitor lifted his arm, and she dutifully turned and stepped beneath it. She found herself gazing into Romeo's soulful brown eyes. Juliet trembled. Paris guided her back into the circle, noticing nothing. When the music stopped, Juliet excused herself and sped across the room. A moment later, she felt fingertips brush her palm.

Romeo and Juliet slowly lifted their masks. Romeo raised Juliet's hand as if holding a precious treasure. "If I profane with my unworthiest hand this holy shrine," he said, referring to Juliet's hand, "the gentle sin is this. My lips, two blushing pilgrims, ready stand to smooth that rough touch with a tender kiss." He kissed her palm.

Juliet laughed in delight. "Good pilgrim, you do wrong your hand too much," she said. "Palm to palm is holy palmers' kiss." The two lovers placed the palms of their hands together.

Romeo looked at their hands. "Dear saint, let lips do what hands do!" He leaned toward her. Juliet closed her eyes and met his lips. For a brief moment, the whole world revolved around that tender kiss.

"Madam!" The couple sprang apart. Juliet's nurse bustled toward them. "Madam, your mother craves a word with you."

Juliet tore herself away.

"Who is her mother?" Romeo asked the nurse.

ROMEO AND JULIET

ROMEO AND JULIET

"The lady of the house," she replied gruffly.

Romeo had almost forgotten where he was—the house of his father's sworn enemy! "Is she a Capulet?" he gasped.

Juliet likewise quizzed her nurse about her mysterious suitor. "His name is Romeo, and a Montague," Nurse answered.

Juliet blanched. "My only love sprung from my only hate!" she cried. After attending to her mother, she retired to her bedchamber.

Romeo slipped outside and scaled the Capulets' high garden wall. Perhaps he would catch a glimpse of Juliet. If nothing else, he could stay near her.

"But soft! What light through yonder window breaks?" Romeo whispered, looking up. Juliet stepped out onto her balcony. "It is the east, and Juliet is the sun! It is my lady; O! It is my love."

Juliet looked up at the round, glowing moon. Before the next full moon, her father expected an answer from her about Paris. Of course she could not marry him, but what would she tell her father— that she had fallen in love with the son of his great enemy? What chance did she have of even seeing Romeo again, given the hate between their families?

"O Romeo, Romeo!" Juliet sighed. "Wherefore art thou Romeo? 'Tis but thy name that is my enemy. O, be some other name! That which we call a rose by any other name would smell as sweet." She smiled to herself. "Refuse thy name, and for that name, which is no part of thee, take all myself."

Romeo stepped out from the shadow of a tree. "I take thee at thy word. Call me but love. Henceforth I never will be Romeo!"

Juliet's heart leaped to see the young Montague.

"Lady, by yonder blessed moon I vow my love," Romeo called to her.

Juliet looked up at the moon. Tomorrow it would be less full than it was tonight. "O, swear not by the moon, the inconstant moon, that monthly changes in her circled orbit."

"What shall I swear by?" asked Romeo.

"Do not swear at all," Juliet replied. She heard her nurse call from within. She would have to act quickly. "If thy bent of love be honorable, thy purpose marriage, send me word tomorrow—where and what time thou wilt perform the rite. Then all my fortunes at thy foot I'll lay and follow thee throughout the world."

Romeo placed both hands on his heart in promise: "So thrive my soul." Juliet wished him a thousand good nights.

At daybreak, Romeo hurried to find his friend and tutor, Friar Laurence. The friar was tending his herb garden, gathering plants for medicines and potions. Only yesterday, he had endured one of Romeo's lengthy laments about Rosaline. Today, Romeo asked to be wed to another girl. Friar Laurence was shocked. His first instinct was to refuse. But when the holy man heard the girl was Lord Capulet's daughter, he had a new thought.

"For this one purpose I'll thy assistant be," Friar Laurence told

Romeo. "That this alliance may so happy prove to turn your households' hatred to pure love."

Romeo sent word to Juliet through her nurse. Juliet slipped away to a small chapel where the friar performed the sacred marriage ceremony. Then Juliet hurried home, lest her parents miss her and discover the marriage too soon. But the pain of parting was softened by anticipation. After darkness fell, Romeo would climb to Juliet's bedroom, where they would spend their wedding night.

Romeo hoped to pass the long hours until then in the company of friends. He headed for a shaded square where Benvolio and Mercutio often spent hot summer days. There, he found his friends arguing with Tybalt.

Tybalt was Juliet's cousin—and so now was Romeo's as well. Romeo resolved to settle the dispute peacefully. Yet as soon as Tybalt saw Romeo, he drew his sword, yelling, "Romeo, thou art a villain."

Romeo kept his sword sheathed. Later, when Tybalt learned of his marriage, he would surely understand. "I do protest I never injured thee," Romeo replied, turning his back. "I love thee better than thou knows."

Mercutio could not believe Romeo was walking away from Tybalt's challenge. "O dishonorable, vile submission!" he exclaimed. Mercutio drew his sword and pointed it at Tybalt. "Come on, rat catcher!" he challenged.

Blade met clanging blade as the two fought. Romeo slipped

between his new cousin and his friend to try to stop their fighting. "Hold Tybalt! Good Mercutio!" he called.

Tybalt, red with rage, thrust his sword under Romeo's arm. It pierced Mercutio.

Mercutio stumbled backward. He looked from Romeo to Tybalt and back again. "A plague on both your houses!" he cried. "They have made worms' meat of me." Mercutio dropped to his knees, then fell dead.

Furious, Romeo turned on Tybalt and drew his own weapon.

"Mercutio's soul is but a little way above our heads, staying for thine to keep him company," he shouted. "Either thou or I, or both, must go with him."

Tybalt sneered. "It will be thou, wretched boy."

Tybalt was the better swordsman, but Romeo had guilt and fury on his side. He fought wildly until at last his sword found its mark. Tybalt was slain.

"Romeo, be gone!" Benvolio urged him. "The prince will doom thee to death if thou art taken."

Romeo fled to Friar Laurence's cell. He asked the friar to go back to the square to see what news he could gather. After a short time, Friar Laurence returned. "I bring thee tidings of the prince's doom," he said. "Not death, but from Verona art thou banished."

Romeo sank to his knees. "Be merciful, say 'death'!" he groaned. "Heaven is here, where Juliet lives."

ROMEO AND JULIET

ROMEO AND JULIET

Suddenly, there was a fierce pounding on the door. Friar Laurence opened it a crack. Juliet's nurse pushed her way in. She clucked at Romeo to stand up and stop crying. "Even so lies Juliet, blubbering and weeping, weeping and blubbering. First for murdered Tybalt calls, and then on Romeo cries."

Romeo had not dared to hope that Juliet might need him. He wiped his eyes and scrambled to his feet.

"Go get thee to thy love," the friar told him. "Tomorrow thou shalt 'scape to Mantua, where thou shalt live till we can find a time to proclaim your marriage, beg pardon of the prince, and call thee back." Friar Laurence dug out an old cloak for a disguise, and Romeo slipped into the dusk.

That night, the lovers lay in each other's arms. Romeo and Juliet wasted no more time weeping over their bad fortune. The young bride and groom imagined their bed a perfect world and shut the curtains against the coming morn.

As dawn broke, birdsong startled them awake. Romeo pushed aside the bed curtains. "It is the lark, the herald of the morn," he said sadly. "I must be gone and live, or stay and die."

There was a quick knock on the door. The nurse burst in. "Madam! Your lady mother is coming to your chamber!"

Romeo kissed his young wife, then scrambled out the window.

"Ho, daughter! Are you up?" Lady Capulet frowned at her daughter's tear-filled eyes. "Evermore weeping for your cousin's death? Thy father, to put thee from thy sorrow, hath set for thee a sudden day of joy. Early next Thursday morn the gallant, young, and noble Count Paris shall, at Saint Peter's Church, happily make thee there a joyful bride."

Juliet was horrified. She thought she had a month to pretend to consider Paris, time enough for her marriage with Romeo to come to light. "He shall not make me there a joyful bride!" she blurted out. "I wonder at this haste!"

Lord Capulet stood in the doorway. He was furious when he heard Juliet's reaction. "Go with Paris to St. Peter's Church on Thursday," he commanded his daughter. "If not, you may hang, beg, starve, die in the streets!"

Juliet was frantic. She appealed to her mother. Lady Capulet snapped, "I have done with thee!"

Juliet's parents stormed out of the room. She huddled against her nurse like a frightened child. "What say'st thou?" she asked. "Some comfort, nurse, I pray."

The nurse loved Juliet, but she was a practical woman. Romeo was handsome, the nurse thought, but handsome fades. What kind of life could the couple have, cut off from their families and banished to Mantua? She stroked Juliet's hair. "I think it best you married Count Paris. O, he's a lovely gentleman! Romeo's a dishcloth compared to him."

Juliet blinked back fresh tears. If her nurse, the person she had always depended upon, did not honor her love for Romeo, she must find help elsewhere. Juliet pretended to take her nurse's advice. "Tell my mother, having displeased my father, I am gone to Friar Laurence to ask for forgiveness."

Juliet burst into the friar's workshop.

"Past hope, past cure, past help!" she cried.

Friar Laurence knew what troubled the girl. Paris had already come to him to arrange their marriage.

"I do spy a kind of hope," the friar said. He unlocked a wooden cabinet. He fished out a small vial filled with a dark brown potion and handed it to Juliet.

"Be merry, give consent to marry Paris on Thursday," the holy man said to Juliet. "But on Wednesday night, take this vial and drink it off." Friar Laurence explained that the potion would give her the appearance of death—no breath, no pulse, stiff limbs. Juliet's family would then lay her to rest in the Capulet crypt. The following night she would awaken to find Friar Laurence and her beloved Romeo at her side. The couple could then flee to Mantua.

Juliet gratefully took the potion and left. The friar composed a letter to Romeo and gave it to a messenger for speedy delivery.

Once home, Juliet did as the friar bid. Lord Capulet was so delighted at Juliet's new obedience that he moved the wedding forward to the next morning.

That night Juliet climbed the stairs to her bedchamber, clutching the friar's vial. Fear and doubt filled her mind: What if the foul-smelling liquid killed her? What if she awoke too soon and found herself surrounded by rotting corpses? Neither was as bad, she decided, as living without her husband. "Romeo, I drink to thee," Juliet pledged and swallowed the potion.

When the nurse entered her chamber the next morning, Juliet lay cold, pale, and still. The household's joy turned to despair. The wedding musicians played a funeral dirge as the Capulets bore the young girl's body to the crypt.

A Montague servant who was Romeo's loyal friend heard of Juliet's death. He borrowed a horse and sped to Mantua with the news. Meanwhile, the messenger carrying the friar's letter to Romeo was delayed by officials. Romeo received no word of Friar Laurence's plan—he heard only of Juliet's death. Anguished, Romeo vowed, "Juliet, I will lie with thee tonight." He bought a wrenching iron and a dose of powerful poison. Then he rode straightaway to Verona.

Romeo entered the graveyard under cover of night. He pried open the doors of the Capulet crypt. He was so intent that he did not see Count Paris, who had come to mourn Juliet.

"This is that banished haughty Montague that murdered Juliet's cousin—with which grief it is supposed the fair creature died," Paris said. "And here he's come to do some villainous shame to the dead bodies!" He rushed at Romeo with sword drawn.

"Tempt not a desperate man!" Romeo warned. "O, be gone!"

But Paris insisted on a fight. Romeo quickly got the upper hand.

"I am slain!" Paris cried. "If thou be merciful, lay me with Juliet."

"In faith, I will," Romeo promised. "Thou art writ with me in sour misfortune's book." He lifted Paris's body as gently as he could and laid it at Juliet's feet.

Romeo held his lantern over Juliet's face. "O my love! My wife! Death hath had no power yet upon thy beauty." He kissed her cold lips, then lay beside her. "Here will I remain with worms that are thy chambermaids." Romeo uncorked his poison. "Here's to my love!" He closed his eyes and drained the bottle. The poison was quick. Romeo kissed Juliet again. "Thus, with a kiss, I die."

A moment later, Friar Laurence appeared. He had just learned that Romeo's letter had been delayed and had rushed to be with Juliet when she awoke. He eyed the open crypt door and blood-stained entrance. "Who's there?" he called. The friar crept in and recoiled in horror. "Romeo! O, pale! Who else? What, Paris, too?" The friar's voice roused Juliet. She awoke as if from a lazy afternoon nap. "O comforting friar! Where is my husband?"

Loud cries and shouts rang out. Juliet sat bolt upright. A single glance told her that the friar's plan had gone terribly wrong.

"Stay not to question, the watchmen are coming!" the terrified friar urged. He grabbed Juliet's hand to lead her away. She shook it loose. Friar Laurence fled into the night.

Juliet knelt down. She found Romeo's bottle and lifted it to her lips. "O churl," she said fondly. "Drunk all, and left no friendly drop to help me after? I will kiss thy lips. Perhaps some poison yet doth hang on them."

The voices outside grew louder.

Juliet drew Romeo's knife and aimed it at her heart. "Oh happy dagger! This is thy sheath. There rust and let me die." With a swift motion, she stabbed herself and collapsed beside her husband.

The cries of the watchmen alarmed the city. The Montagues and the Capulets rushed to the crypt. So did the prince. Friar Laurence returned and told the tragic tale of the star-crossed lovers.

"See what a scourge is laid upon your hate," the prince admonished the two families. "Heaven finds means to kill your joys with love."

Lord Capulet offered his hand to Lord Montague in peace. They vowed to raise a pair of golden statues to honor their children—and to remind all that never was there a story of more woe than this of Juliet and her Romeo.

TWELFTH NIGHT

Viola, a young noblewoman, is shipwrecked and stranded in a foreign land. She fears her twin brother, Sebastian, is drowned. The plucky young woman dresses as a boy and becomes a servant in a duke's court—and immediately finds herself in a love triangle with the duke and a beautiful countess. The confusion is compounded by a snobby steward, an eccentric uncle, a sea captain, a scheming maid, and a miracle: Sebastian lives!

Illustration by Chesley McLaren

THE MAIN PLAYERS

VIOLA, *a young noblewoman disguised as a boy, later called* CESARIO

SEBASTIAN, *Viola's twin brother*

ORSINO, *Duke of Illyria*

OLIVIA, *a countess*

MARIA, *Olivia's serving woman*

MALVOLIO, *Olivia's steward*

SIR TOBY BELCH, *Olivia's drunken uncle*

SIR ANDREW AGUECHEEK, *Sir Toby's foolish friend and Olivia's suitor*

ANTONIO, *a sea captain*

THE TIME & PLACE

EARLY 17TH CENTURY, ILLYRIA, A COUNTRY ON THE ADRIATIC SEA

Stones scraped the rowboat's wooden hull as a pair of sailors steadied the vessel. Viola gathered her skirts, which were torn and tattered from the storm, and prepared to disembark. The young noblewoman hesitated. She turned to watch the roiling waves, which had destroyed her ship and drowned her twin brother, Sebastian. At last she took the hand of the captain who had rescued her and stepped onto the unfamiliar shore.

"What country is this, friend?" Viola asked. "Who governs here?"

"This is Illyria," the captain replied. "It is ruled by Orsino, a noble duke. Orsino seeks the love of fair Olivia. She is the daughter of a count that died some twelve months past. Her brother shortly also died, for whose dear love, they say, Olivia hath forsworn the company of men."

Viola considered her situation. She was of noble birth, but a foreigner in an unknown land. She was a woman alone, with no friends or family. She had only a small purse of gold coins, all she'd been able to rescue from the shipwreck.

Then she had a brilliant and bold idea: She'd disguise herself as a boy. As a boy, Viola could move around freely. She could work as a servant and find out more about this island. Then she could safely reveal her identity and ask for help.

"I'll serve this duke," Viola decided. She fished in her purse for a gold coin and offered it to the captain. She asked him to buy her some boy's clothes. "Conceal me what I am," Viola told the captain.

TWELFTH NIGHT

TWELFTH NIGHT

"Present me as a serving boy to the duke. I can sing and speak to him in many sorts of music that will allow me very worth his service." Viola announced she would go by the male name Cesario.

A few days later, Duke Orsino lay on a couch in the royal palace. He was so lovesick he didn't want to do anything but think about Olivia. His musicians played a melancholy song to match their lord's mood.

When the tune ended, Orsino sighed. "If music be the food of love, play on," he said. He sighed again and thought of his beloved Olivia, who did not return his affection.

"Enough, no more." the duke said. He waved his musicians away. "'Tis not so sweet now as it was before."

The duke called for his new page, Cesario. The youth had turned up at his palace a few days before. Orsino had taken quite a liking to the page. Cesario proved to be excellent company. He was sensitive, understanding, and could sing beautifully. The youth's quick wit, Orsino decided, more than compensated for a notable lack in the masculine arts of fencing and hunting. The duke teased Cesario about his soft, beardless skin—but he never suspected his young page was female!

The young woman pretending to be a young man surprised herself: Viola, as Cesario, felt freer than she ever had been. And the duke's good company had something to do with this happiness.

One morning, Duke Orsino found a new task for Cesario. "Good youth, go to Olivia and unfold the passion of my love," the duke told his young servant.

Cesario was taken aback. "I'll do my best to woo your lady," she stammered and left to seek the countess. "But whoever I woo," Cesario said to herself, "myself, Viola, would be thy wife."

Olivia listlessly wandered through her palace, mourning her brother. Her self-important steward, Malvolio, strutted behind her like a rooster guarding a hen. Malvolio pecked at anyone who came near, especially Olivia's uncle, Sir Toby Belch, whose drunken requests for money were always ill timed. Sir Toby usually had his ridiculous, but rich, friend Sir Andrew Aguecheek in tow. Aguecheek did his clumsy best to woo Olivia, whenever he got to see her . . . which wasn't often!

The last thing Olivia wanted was yet another love poem from the persistent Orsino. But when Cesario arrived, he was so witty that Olivia relented and ordered a servant to usher in the boy. She and her waiting women would play a little game with this cheeky youth.

Cesario entered Olivia's chamber and found six women covered in veils waiting for him. The page had no idea which one was the countess. Cesario eyed the veiled women nervously. They hooted with laughter.

"The honorable lady of the house, which is she?" Cesario asked.

"Speak to me, I shall answer for her," said Olivia, still disguised.

TWELFTH NIGHT

"Give me assurance that you be the lady of the house," Cesario said. "I would be loath to cast away my speech, for it is excellently well penned."

"Are you a comedian?" asked Olivia.

"No," answered Cesario. "But I am not what I play."

Cesario and Olivia bantered back and forth. The countess found herself drawn to the young page. She ordered her waiting women to leave her alone with him. When Cesario asked her to lift her veil, she did so. The youth was awestruck by the countess's beauty. Cesario could see why Duke Orsino was so smitten.

Cesario decided to take a more direct approach. "My lord and master loves you," the page told the countess.

Olivia stood up abruptly, a signal that the audience was over. "Your lord does know my mind. I cannot love him. He might have took his answer long ago."

"Farewell, fair cruelty." Cesario bowed. "Yet if I did love you with my master's flame, with such a suffering . . ." Cesario's voice trailed off. Though disguised as a boy, Viola still had the feelings of a woman. She realized that she loved Orsino and empathized with how deeply Orsino loved Olivia!

The countess was gripped by the passion in Cesario's eyes. "Why, what would you do?"

"Make me a willow cabin at your gate, and cry out 'Olivia!'" Cesario swore. "Write songs of unrequited love and sing them loud even in the dead of night. Oh, you would not rest between air and earth, but you would pity me!" With this, Cesario strode away.

"You might do much," Olivia whispered. Her heart, so heavy since her brother's death, felt as if it would rise out of her chest. "Methinks I feel this youth's perfections with an invisible and subtle stealth to creep in at mine eyes." Cesario had come to beg Olivia to love Orsino, but the youth's beautiful speeches had caused the countess to fall in love with the page instead.

After Cesario left, Olivia became anxious. If Orsino accepted Olivia's rejection of his love, he would never send Cesario as his messenger again. The countess slipped a ring off her finger and called for Malvolio. Olivia told her steward that Cesario had given her the ring as a gift from the duke. "Tell him I'll none of it," the countess said. She ordered her steward to run after Cesario, give him the ring, and tell him to come by tomorrow for her explanation. Malvolio caught Cesario at the edge of the palace grounds. "Countess Olivia returns this ring to you, sir." He threw the ring at Cesario's feet and stalked away.

"I left no ring with her. What means this lady?" Cesario's eyes grew wide. An awful thought occurred to the page: "She loves me, sure. Fortune forbid my boy's disguise have not charmed her! Poor lady, she were better love a dream. And yet, how on earth will this turn out? I love Orsino, Orsino loves Olivia, and Olivia loves me!"

Late that night, while Olivia was indeed dreaming of Cesario,

TWELFTH NIGHT

Sir Toby and Sir Andrew were drinking to each other's health in the countess's hall. Their drunken singing echoed through the palace.

Olivia's serving woman, Maria, did not want to see Sir Toby in his niece's bad graces. She wanted him to marry her, but Sir Toby had little interest in anything but drinking and carousing. "For the love o' God, peace!" Maria urged. Sir Toby just laughed and charmed her into uncorking a new bottle of wine.

A moment later Malvolio swept in. He would teach them a lesson. He had prepared a little speech . . . and was clearly going to enjoy delivering it!

"Sir Toby," the pompous steward began, "my lady bade me tell you that if you can separate yourself and your misdemeanors, you are welcome to the house. If not, she is very willing to bid you farewell."

"Push off," Sir Toby swore.

"Mistress Maria, serve them no more drink," Malvolio commanded. Then, with a self-satisfied smirk, he departed.

Sir Toby made a drunken effort to draw his sword. But Maria thought quickly about how she could turn this to her advantage. She promised more entertaining revenge—to be enacted on the morrow.

The next morning, Duke Orsino ordered Cesario to return to Olivia with another vow of love.

"But if she cannot love you, sir?" Cesario asked.

Orsino frowned. "I cannot be so answered."

"Sooth, but you must. Say that some lady hath for your love as great a pang of heart as you have for Olivia," Cesario said. "You cannot love her. You tell her so. Must she not then be answered?"

"There is no woman's sides can bide the beating of so strong a passion as love doth give my heart," the duke swore.

Cesario smiled bitterly. How could such a wonderful man say such ridiculous things? Cesario vowed to make Orsino understand how passionately a woman can love.

"My father had a daughter who loved a man, the same way, were I a woman, I should love your lordship," Cesario said. "She never told her love, but pined in thought," the youth added.

"But died thy sister of her love, my boy?" asked Orsino.

"I am all the daughters of my father's house," Cesario said boldly and waited for the duke to decipher this riddle. Orsino looked at the page blankly.

Cesario sighed. "Sir, shall I to this lady, then?"

"Ay, to her in haste," the duke replied. "Give her this jewel. Say my love will not be denied."

Meanwhile, unbeknownst to Cesario, Sebastian was striding into town with Antonio, a famous sea captain who had rescued him.

Antonio warily scanned the streets for soldiers. He had made an enemy of Duke Orsino in battle and did not wish to be seen in Illyria. But he also had grown fond of Sebastian and did not want to abandon the young man in a strange land. Antonio offered to find lodgings for them both while Sebastian toured the island's sights.

TWELFTH NIGHT

Knowing that the young man had lost his gold at sea, the captain insisted that Sebastian borrow his ample purse.

A less charitable spirit reigned in Olivia's garden, where Sir Toby and Sir Andrew hid in breathless anticipation. Maria had set a trap for Malvolio—a trap that could be sprung only by the steward's own vanity. The bait was a love note, written by Maria on Countess Olivia's stationery and placed on a garden path where Malvolio often walked. The steward had just discovered the note.

"*'To the unknown beloved'*," Malvolio read aloud. His eyebrows shot up. Could this be the sign he had been hoping for? Could this letter be from Countess Olivia? Malvolio eagerly ripped the seal.

"*'I may command where I adore'*," he read.

"Why, she may command me: I serve her," Malvolio cried.

He read on. "*'In my stars I am above thee. But be not afraid of greatness. Some are born great, some achieve greatness, and some have greatness thrust upon 'em'!*" The haughty steward puffed out his chest even further. Surely Olivia meant to thrust greatness upon him by marrying him and, in so doing, make him Count Malvolio!

He greedily read the rest of the letter. The writer wished her beloved to wear bright yellow stockings held up by elaborate cross-gartering and to smile whenever he was in her sight. Malvolio strutted away, a ghoulish grin stretched across his face. He was eager to fulfill the letter's commands without delay.

Sir Toby and Sir Andrew tumbled out of their hiding place, shaking with laughter. As they brushed themselves off, a servant passed by, leading Cesario to Olivia. Sir Andrew scrambled after them, anxious to eavesdrop on the suit of his rival Orsino. But Olivia took Cesario's arm and shut the door firmly in Sir Andrew's face.

Inside the palace, Cesario twisted out of Olivia's grasp. "Madam, I come to whet your gentle thoughts on Duke Orsino's behalf."

"I pray you, never speak again of him," Olivia cried. "I did send a ring in chase of you. What might you think?"

Cesario took the ring from her pocket and placed it in Olivia's palm. "You'll send nothing, madam, to my lord?"

"Cesario!" Tears of frustration blurred Olivia's vision. "I love thee so, that, despite all thy pride, neither wit nor reason can my passion hide."

Cesario searched for words that would discourage Olivia but not insult her. "I have one heart and that no woman has, nor never one shall mistress be of it." Cesario departed with an awkward bow.

Olivia, like Orsino, refused to take no for an answer. She sent a servant to bring Cesario back again.

While Olivia waited, Malvolio burst in upon her, grinning from ear to ear. He patted the pocket that contained Maria's letter. "Its commands shall be executed," he told the countess. Malvolio displayed a yellow leg festooned with ribbons. He winked and blew kisses at the countess.

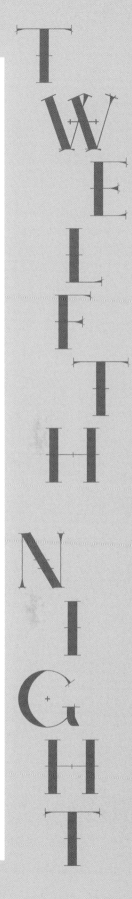

TWELFTH NIGHT

TWELFTH NIGHT

"Are you mad?" the startled lady asked. "'Some have greatness thrust upon them!'" Malvolio crowed. He moved toward the countess.

Olivia jumped back. "Heaven restore thee!" she exclaimed.

Maria entered with the news that Cesario had returned.

Olivia cast a worried glance at her grinning steward. "Good Maria, let this fellow be looked to. Where's my uncle Toby?" The countess hurried away. Maria summoned Olivia's uncle.

Sir Toby looked at Malvolio spitefully. "Come, we'll have him in a dark room and bound," he whispered to Maria. "My niece is already in the belief that he's mad."

Maria uneasily agreed. With the help of some other servants, she and Sir Toby dragged Malvolio down to the basement and locked him in. When they returned to the main hall, they found Sir Andrew dressed in traveling gear.

Sir Andrew frowned petulantly at Sir Toby. "I saw your niece do more favors to the duke's serving-man than ever she bestowed upon me," he complained. Sir Andrew swore he would leave at once.

Sir Toby Belch had no intention of letting Sir Andrew Aguecheek—and his generous purse—depart. He easily convinced his foolish friend that Olivia had shown preference to Cesario in order to test Sir Andrew's honor and make him jealous. By the time Sir Toby was finished talking, Sir Andrew was resolved: He would challenge Cesario to a duel!

When Cesario burst out of the palace, ears ringing with Olivia's declarations of love, Sir Toby grabbed the youth's collar.

"Of what nature the wrongs are thou hast done him, I know not," said Sir Toby. "But Sir Andrew, bloodthirsty as the hunter, waits for thee at the orchard end."

Cesario begged Sir Toby to broker a peace; the page had no idea how to fight a duel. Instead, Sir Toby told Sir Andrew that his young rival was hungry for a fight. Within minutes, Sir Toby had driven the two together, swords drawn and knees knocking.

Suddenly, a figure jumped between the two, his weapon aimed at Sir Andrew. "If this young gentleman have done offence," he said, gesturing at Cesario, "I take the fault on me."

Cesario was grateful, but confused: Why was this man willing to so risk his life? In fact, the stranger was Antonio, the captain. He had mistaken Cesario for Sebastian.

Before Cesario could speak, however, Antonio was set upon by Orsino's officers. They had recognized him as an enemy of the duke and tracked him to the orchard.

As the officers bound his hands, Antonio realized how useful it would be to have his money right this moment. Still thinking he addressed Sebastian, Antonio turned to Cesario. "I must entreat of you some of that money."

"What money, sir?" Cesario asked.

Antonio could not believe his friend would betray him thus. "Will you deny me now?" he cried as the soldiers dragged him away. "The money I gave you but half an hour since! Oh heavens themselves!"

A little hope crept into Cesario's heart. "Prove true, imagination, O prove true, that I, dear brother, be now taken for you!" Cesario ran toward Orsino's palace. The duke would surely help. If he freed Antonio, the captain could be further questioned about Sebastian.

Sir Andrew watched Cesario's retreating figure. His shallow courage returned. "I'll after him and beat him," the foolish man declared.

It was Sir Andrew's bad luck to find not Cesario, but Sebastian, who had wandered there in search of Antonio. "Now, sir, have I met you again?" Sir Andrew said pompously. "There's for you." He punched Sebastian.

Sebastian returned the blow with interest. "Why, there's for thee, and there, and there."

Hearing Sir Andrew's screams, Sir Toby barreled in and grabbed Sebastian from behind. A moment later, Olivia arrived and angrily shooed her uncle and the others away.

Olivia took Sebastian's arm tenderly. "Be not offended, dear Cesario."

"Either I am mad, or else this is a dream," Sebastian whispered. He looked at Olivia's lovely face. "If it be thus to dream, still let me sleep!"

Olivia was surprised by Cesario's seeming change of heart. He wasn't pushing her away as he had in the past. Sebastian could not fathom what was going on in the least. But he didn't care; this was bliss!

Afraid that Cesario might change again, Olivia proposed that they immediately go to a chapel and be married. They could hold a more elaborate ceremony later, she thought.

With a happy laugh, Sebastian agreed. If he could spend his life with Olivia, what did it matter if she called him "Cesario"? The two went hand in hand to the chapel.

Not long after, Cesario brought Duke Orsino to where Antonio was being held.

"What foolish boldness brought thee to thine enemies?" Orsino asked the captain.

Antonio spat. "That most ungrateful boy there by your side, who from the rude sea's enraged and foamy mouth did I redeem . . ." But before he could finish, Olivia suddenly swept in. The duke was over-joyed. Here at last was his love!

Olivia ignored the duke and went straight over to his page.

"Cesario, you do not keep promise with me," Olivia said.

The lady's familiar tone embarrassed Cesario. "My *lord* would speak," the page answered.

Olivia's loving gaze never left Cesario even as she addressed Orsino. "If it be the old tune, my lord, it is to mine ear as howling after music."

"Still so cruel?" Orsino asked.

"Still so constant, lord," Olivia corrected.

Orsino glared at Cesario, who had become so dear to him. Clearly, Olivia had fallen in love with this fine-featured lad. In his anger, the duke vowed he would kill Cesario rather than let Olivia marry him. "I'll sacrifice the lamb that I do love, to spite a raven's heart within a dove," the duke swore.

Cesario looked up at Orsino with a full heart. "And I for you a thousand deaths would die." When Orsino turned on his heel and left, Cesario followed, mind racing. If the duke made good on his deadly vow, would he find Viola beneath the disguise—and realize how she had loved him?

"Cesario, husband, stay!" Olivia called.

Orsino stopped short. "*Husband?*" Anger, then sorrow, passed over his face. "Farewell," the duke told Cesario. "Direct thy feet where thou and I may henceforth never meet."

"My lord, I do protest. . . ." Cesario cried.

At this moment, Sir Andrew bumbled in, bloody from another unsuccessful attack on Sebastian. "For the love of God, a surgeon! And send one for Sir Toby!" Sir Andrew stopped short when he saw Cesario. "You broke my head for nothing."

"I never hurt you!" Cesario insisted.

As Cesario argued with Sir Andrew, Sebastian ran in and took Olivia by the hand. "I am sorry, madam, I have hurt your kinsman," he said.

Stunned, Olivia looked from one Cesario to the other.

Sebastian's attention was on Orsino's prisoner. "Antonio! How have the hours tortured me since I have lost thee!" he cried.

"How have you made division of yourself?" Antonio replied. "An apple, cleft in two, is not more twin that these two creatures. Which is Sebastian?"

Sebastian and Cesario stood face-to-face. They looked like a man and his mirror.

"I had a sister whom the blind waves devoured," Sebastian said. "I never had a brother. What kin are you to me? What parentage?" he asked Cesario.

"Sebastian was my father. He had a mole upon his brow."

"So had mine," Sebastian said.

"My father died when I was thirteen years old," Cesario added.

"*My* father finished his mortal act the day my sister turned thirteen," Sebastian replied.

"I had a brother who went to a watery grave," said Cesario. "If spirits can assume form, you come to frighten us."

Sebastian assured her he was no ghost. Cesario laughed with joy. It was true! This was Sebastian. Now, Cesario could become Viola once again. She threw off her boy's hat and launched herself into her brother's arms.

"Thrice-welcome, drowned Viola!" Sebastian cried.

In short time, Sebastian understood that it was his sister who

TWELFTH NIGHT

had won him a wife. He turned apologetically to Olivia. "So comes it, lady, you have been mistook."

Olivia threw her arms around Sebastian, then smiled at Viola. "A sister!" The women laughed and embraced.

Still, Viola did not dare look at Orsino. The duke turned her around slowly and searched her face. "Boy, thou hast said to me a thousand times thou never shouldst love woman like to me."

"And all those sayings will I over-swear," Viola declared.

The duke laughed at all they had shared and at how quickly his fondness for the boy could turn to love for the woman. "Give me thy hand," the duke said to Viola. "Let me see thee in thy woman's weeds."

Viola explained that the sea captain who had rescued her had her clothes. She had heard the captain was being held in prison on an unknown matter at Malvolio's request. Olivia called at once for her steward. Malvolio was hauled up from the basement, dirty, disheveled, and indignant.

"Madam, you have done me wrong!" Malvolio thrust a soiled paper at Olivia. "Pray you, peruse that letter. You must not now deny it is your handwriting."

Olivia read the letter and understood at once what had happened. "Alas, Malvolio, this is not my writing; 'tis Maria's hand."

The countess called for Sir Toby and Maria and promised Malvolio he could help decide their punishment. It was too late. Maria had finally gotten her wish. A friend stepped forward to say that the pair had eloped. Malvolio, humiliated and unforgiving, stormed away.

Olivia decided to make peace with Malvolio later. For the moment, the four lovers had a double wedding feast to celebrate—and the sooner the better!

Orsino clapped the boy's cap back onto Viola's head. "Cesario, come," the duke laughed. "For so you shall be, while you are a man. But when in women's clothing you are seen, Orsino's mistress and his fancy's queen!"

KING LEAR

A king gives up a throne. Daughters flatter and deceive a father. A father disowns a beloved daughter. Wife plots against husband. Brother turns against brother. Sisters pursue jealousy to the death. *King Lear* explores a chilling family truth: The deepest wounds can be inflicted by the dearest hands.

Illustration by Leo and Diane Dillon

175

KING LEAR

THE MAIN PLAYERS

LEAR, *King of Britain*

GONERIL, *Lear's oldest daughter*

DUKE OF ALBANY, *Goneril's husband*

REGAN, *Lear's middle daughter*

DUKE OF CORNWALL, *Regan's husband*

CORDELIA, *Lear's youngest daughter*

EARL OF KENT, *Lear's faithful advisor*

EARL OF GLOUCESTER, *Lear's chief nobleman*

EDGAR, *Gloucester's older son*

EDMUND, *Gloucester's younger son*

FOOL, *the king's court jester*

THE TIME & PLACE

ANCIENT BRITAIN

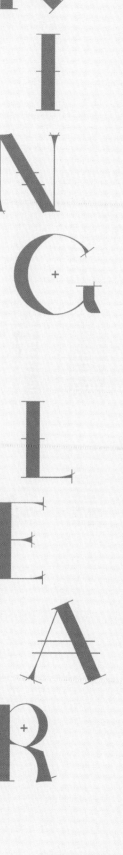

King Lear unrolled a map of his empire and ran a gnarled finger along its newest markings. He had spent decades keeping peace in the land. Now the king was old and tired. He had decided to divide his kingdom amongst his three daughters, Goneril, Regan, and Cordelia. He would leave governing to them and remain king in title only.

Lear intended to give his eldest daughter, Goneril, and his middle daughter, Regan, each a part of his kingdom equal in size and riches. The third portion he now lingered over. It was larger, lovelier, and more fertile than the other two. Lear had carved it out for his favorite daughter, Cordelia. She was the youngest but the wisest and most good-natured of all three women, and so would make the best ruler. Cordelia was today to be betrothed to either the Duke of Burgundy or the King of France. This meant she would live much of the time across the sea, ruling from afar. Lear couldn't bear to be parted from Cordelia. He planned to live out his days with her. It was best to divide the kingdom now.

To make the divisions appear equitable, the king proposed a test of his daughters' devotion. He called together his royal court, Cordelia's suitors, and summoned his three daughters. King Lear announced that he would divide his land according to how well his children publicly proclaimed their love for him. Lear was confident that sweet, loyal Cordelia's answer would prove the best.

"Which of you shall we say doth love us the most?" the king asked.

KING LEAR

Goneril spoke first, her hands clasped to her heart. "Sir, I love you more than word can wield the matter," she cried. "Dearer than eyesight, space, and liberty, no less than life!"

Regan stepped in front of her older sister. "She comes too short. I profess myself an enemy to all other joys," she declared.

Lear turned eagerly to Cordelia. "What can you say to draw a third more opulent than your sisters?"

Cordelia was silent. She loved her father dearly, but thought his test was wrong. She could not join her sisters in their self-serving flattery. She struggled over her answer. "Nothing, my lord," she said at last.

The old king felt the blood rise in his wrinkled face. "Nothing will come of nothing. Speak again."

"Good my lord, you have begot me, bred me, loved me. I return these duties back as are right fit. I obey you, love you, and most honor you." Cordelia looked at Goneril and Regan, who stood with their husbands, the Dukes of Albany and Cornwall. "Why have my sisters taken husbands if they say they love you all?"

Cornelia's answer was truthful, but painful and humiliating. Lear was a man accustomed to hearing what he wished to hear. "Truth be thy dowry," the king thundered. Then Lear drew his dagger, slashed his map, and sliced Cordelia's portion in two. One half he added to Goneril's land, the other half to Regan's inheritance. Then the king coldly turned to Cordelia. "As a stranger to my heart

I hold thee forever," he said. "Better thou hadst not been born than not to have pleased me better."

Cordelia's eyes filled with tears, but she held her head high.

The Earl of Kent, Lear's most faithful advisor, could remain silent no longer. He knew it was his duty to protect the king, even from himself. "Thy youngest daughter does not love thee least," the loyal earl objected. "Revoke thy gift; I'll tell thee thou dost evil."

Kent's words heaped fuel on Lear's fiery anger. "Out of my sight!" he railed and banished the earl from the kingdom, on pain of death.

Lear then called forth two suitors who had been wooing Cordelia and asked if either would marry her without a dowry. The Duke of Burgundy dropped his suit at once. But the King of France was impressed by Cordelia's honesty, and said he loved her more than ever and would make her his queen.

"Take her!" King Lear shouted and swept out of the throne room.

As the rest of the royal party followed Lear, the Earl of Gloucester stood stunned by the king's rashness. The earl was one of the highest nobles in the land. He had never seen his king behave like this. It disturbed him. Gloucester also thought about his own two sons: Edgar by his wife and Edmund, slightly younger, by his mistress. Gloucester was confident that nothing would ever drive a wedge between him and either of his sons . . . or could any man's children turn against him?

KING LEAR

Unbeknownst to the earl, Edmund was indeed at that moment scheming to get his father's land. He planned to turn his father against Edgar. With the elder son out of the way, Edmund, the younger son, would inherit Gloucester's title and property.

Edmund strode into the throne room, reading a letter. When he was sure that his father had seen it, he hurriedly shoved the note into his doublet.

Gloucester smiled. This letter must reveal some mischief. Was it a love letter? He laughingly asked Edmund to hand it over.

"I beseech you, sir," Edmund replied. "It is a letter from my brother that I have not all read; and for so much as I have, I find it not fit for you."

Gloucester's smile disappeared. He demanded to see the message. Edmund sighed and handed over the letter, which he had forged to look like Edgar's handwriting. Gloucester's eyes widened. Here was evidence that Edgar, anxious to get his inheritance, was plotting against his own father's life!

The old earl was devastated. He ordered Edmund to find out more about his older brother's intentions and report back to him.

Edmund nodded. Everything had gone just as he had planned. He sought out Edgar and, professing brotherly loyalty, warned him that their father was in a murderous rage against him for unknown reasons. Edmund urged Edgar to go into hiding. He promised he would intercede with their father on Edgar's behalf. Edgar was

bewildered by this strange warning, but believed his brother and fled into the countryside.

Within a week, King Lear had installed himself at Goneril's castle. He brought with him 100 boisterous knights and a court fool. The king and his followers spent their days hunting and their nights feasting and merrymaking. They wore out the castle servants—and Goneril's patience.

"Our court shows like a riotous inn," Goneril told her father. She instructed her servants to ignore the commands of the old king and his followers. Now that she owned one half of the kingdom, Goneril swelled with her new power. She would rule as she saw fit. She ignored the fact that she and her sister had promised to care for their father in his old age.

Lear was shocked by this ill treatment.

"Ingratitude, more hideous in a child than in the sea monster," the king complained to his constant companion, the fool. The fool was not surprised in the least. "Thou hadst little wit in thy bald crown when thou gavest thy golden one away," he clucked. The fool always told the truth—but dressed it up as a joke.

Lear allowed his fool to tease him because he was so certain of the fellow's loyalty. But Goneril's servants were another matter.

One evening, a humbly dressed stranger approached King Lear and asked permission to serve him. The man proved useful at once, taking the inattentive servants to task and even tripping an insolent

KING LEAR

steward. Lear did not recognize his new ally—the banished Earl of Kent, seeking to continue his loyal service in disguise.

Goneril was furious with Lear's new servant and ordered her father to send away fifty of his knights in response.

King Lear trembled with rage. "How sharper than a serpent's tooth it is to have a thankless child! When Regan shall hear this of thee, with her nails she'll flay thy wolfish visage!" He sent Kent ahead with a letter to his middle daughter, telling of Goneril's cruelty and saying he was coming to stay with her. Goneril, too, sent a letter to Regan, telling her version of the story.

Lear stormed out of Goneril's castle. He was overcome by such intense emotion that he feared for his sanity. "O, let me not be mad, sweet heaven!" the king cried to his fool. "Let me not be mad!"

Regan and her husband, the Duke of Cornwall, were already on their way to visit the Earl of Gloucester. Gloucester's castle stood midway between those of Lear's daughters.

The Earl of Kent and Goneril's steward, each bearing a letter, arrived at Gloucester's castle at the same time. When Kent saw the steward present Goneril's treacherous letter to Regan, he lost his temper and attacked the servant. This in turn infuriated Cornwall who promptly had Kent clapped into the stocks as punishment. Gloucester, lord of the castle, was too troubled by his own son Edgar's possible betrayal to intervene.

"These late eclipses in the sun and moon portend no good to us," Gloucester said to himself. Now he anticipated more trouble.

Shortly after, King Lear arrived at Gloucester's castle. He did not even finish his affectionate greeting to Regan before Goneril arrived, too. The king's two older daughters united against him.

"What should you need of more than fifty knights?" Regan asked him. "Yea, or so many? If you will come to me, I entreat you to bring but five-and-twenty. To no more will I give place."

Lear seethed with anger. "I'll go with thee," he said at last to Goneril. "Thy fifty yet doth double five-and-twenty, so thou art twice her love."

Goneril linked arms with Regan. "Why need you five-and-twenty? Ten? Or five?" she taunted.

"What need one?" Regan added.

"You unnatural hags, I will have such revenges on you both!" Lear sputtered. "O fool, I shall go mad!" The king strode angrily out of the castle alone and headed toward the heath. A gathering storm rumbled in the distance. Alarmed for their king's safety, Kent and the fool followed.

A spiteful smile spread across Regan's face. "To willful men the injuries that they themselves procure must be their schoolmasters." She turned to the Earl of Gloucester. "Shut up your doors."

"The bleak winds do sorely ruffle," Gloucester objected.

"By no means entreat the king to stay," Goneril commanded.

KING LEAR

Outside the castle's stone walls, Lear defiantly faced the growing tempest. "Blow, winds, and crack your cheeks!" he cried. "Rage, blow. Rumble thy bellyful. Spit, fire! Spout, rain! The tempest in my mind doth from my senses take all feeling." Lightning flashed and thunder cracked, as if in response.

Having scouted the area, Kent fought his way back through the storm to his king. "Gracious my lord, hard by here is a hovel." Kent took Lear's arm and led him toward the small rough hut.

As they made their way across the desolate heath, Lear squinted into the storm. "Poor naked wretches that bide the pelting of this pitiless storm, how shall your houseless heads and unfed sides defend you?" He remembered all the riches he had enjoyed while so many of his subjects lived in poverty. "O, I have taken too little care of this!" the king realized.

Inside the hovel they discovered a wretched man dressed in nothing but a rough blanket.

"What art thou?" Kent asked.

Beneath the grime and matted hair was Gloucester's good son, Edgar. Thanks to Edmund's lies, Edgar could not flee Britain; soldiers were in every port watching for him. It was much safer to dwell in the shadow of his father's castle. There Edgar called himself "Tom" and pretended to be a lunatic beggar.

"This is poor Tom," Edgar jabbered. "When the foul fiend rages, eats cow-dung for salads, swallows the old rat and the ditch-dog, drinks the green scum of the standing pool." He scratched violently at one ear. "Alow, alow, loo, loo!"

Lear watched in amazement. He felt a similar wildness growing in his mind.

Inside the castle, Gloucester prepared to brave the storm. "If I die for it, the king my old master must be rescued," he confided to his son Edmund. The old earl also said that he had received word that Cordelia and the French army had landed at Dover. They planned to rescue Lear and avenge all insults against him. Disobeying the orders of his royal visitors, Gloucester gathered supplies for the king.

Edmund rushed to tell Goneril and Regan and her husband, Cornwall, all that his father had reported. In gratitude for this treachery, Cornwall denounced Gloucester and gave Edmund his father's title and land. He then directed Edmund to accompany Goneril back to her castle so she could warn her husband, Albany, about the coming French invasion. "The revenges we are bound to take upon your traitorous father are not fit for your beholding," Cornwall told Edmund.

Meanwhile, Gloucester, realizing the daughters wanted their father dead, made his way out of the castle. He headed out across the rain-swept heath in search of his king. He found Lear ranting with a filthy madman in the hovel. Lear pretended to be in a court of law. He made the fool and the madman, Tom, act the part of his

KING LEAR

daughters. Lear put them on trial for their inhuman behavior.

Appalled at the state of his royal lord, Gloucester urged Kent and the fool to carry the now surely mad king toward Dover, where Cordelia's troops would help them. Then Gloucester secretly returned to his own castle.

As soon as he reached the castle gate, two guards seized him. They hauled Gloucester before Regan and Cornwall and bound him to a chair. Regan denounced him as a traitor for helping her father and not reporting the arrival of the French army.

Cornwall towered over the old earl. With malicious pleasure, he gouged out one of Gloucester's eyes. "Out, vile jelly," Cornwall sneered. "Where is thy lustre now?"

"One side will mock the other." Regan laughed cruelly. "The other, too."

Cornwall's servants were shocked by this barbarity. One drew a sword and tried to stop his master. The servant mortally wounded Cornwall, but not before Regan ran him through with a sword.

Cornwall hauled himself to his feet. With great effort, he plucked out Gloucester's other eye.

Gloucester screamed for his younger son. "Edmund, enkindle all the sparks of nature to revenge this horrid act!"

Regan leaned over Gloucester's bloody, unseeing face. "Thou call'st on him that hates thee," she spat. "It was Edmund that made the overture of thy treasons to us." She turned her back. "Go thrust him out at gates, and let him smell his way to Dover," she cried to her servants.

As Regan knelt before her dying husband, an old servant untied Gloucester and led him out of the castle and onto the heath. In short time, they ran into the lunatic beggar, Tom. Gloucester listened to his raving, but did not recognize Tom as his son Edgar. Edgar was anguished to see his father's wounds. He cried out, but in gibberish, still playing the lunatic.

The blind earl knew the old servant with him could not travel far, so he asked the crazy beggar to lead him instead to a high sea cliff in Dover.

As they traveled, Gloucester bemoaned what fate had dealt him. "As flies to wanton boys are we to the gods," the old earl said. "They kill us for their sport."

The blind man and the beggar neared the cliffs of Dover. Edgar, still undetected, saw that his father intended to leap to his death. So he instead brought Gloucester to a low hill and convinced him that the cliff lay below.

"If Edgar live, O bless him!" Gloucester cried. Then he hurled himself forward. The old man fainted before he hit the soft earth.

Edgar gently roused his father and, putting on a different accent, swore that he had seen Gloucester fall from a great height. The old man was astounded that the gods had protected him. He vowed to never again try to take his own life.

Suddenly, a figure burst upon father and son with weapon drawn. "Thou old unhappy traitor, the sword is out that must destroy thee," the intruder cried.

Edgar drew his own blade and planted himself before the man. It was Goneril's steward. Regan, fearing that the blinded earl would stir up sympathy against her, had offered a reward for killing Gloucester.

The steward's greedy ambition far outstripped his talent. Before he landed even one hit, he was struck down by Edgar.

"Bury my body, and give the letters which thou find'st about me to Edmund, Earl of Gloucester," the steward gasped. And with that, he died.

Edgar drew two scrolls from the steward's doublet. They were both addressed to his brother. The first letter was from Regan. Now widowed, she asked Edmund to marry her. The second note was from Goneril. She begged Edmund to kill her husband, Albany, so that she would be free to become Edmund's wife. Edgar pocketed the damning letters.

Suddenly, another figure approached, this one ragged, unarmed, and crowned with weeds. He muttered incessantly.

Gloucester turned an ear toward this man. "Is it not the king?" he asked.

Lear studied the blind man without recognition and giggled. "No eyes in thy head? Get thee glass eyes, and, like a scurvy politician, seem to see the things thou dost not," the mad king taunted.

Shouts rang out in the distance. It was the men under Cordelia's command. Her army had encamped nearby. Before Edgar or Gloucester could stop him, King Lear sprinted away, hollering as if he were hunting a wild animal.

The men at last caught up with Lear and gently ushered him to a bed in Cordelia's tent. There the king slept a peaceful, dreamless sleep while war preparations were made on both sides.

When Lear awoke, he found Cordelia by his side. "Pray you now, forget and forgive," he said to his daughter. "I am old and foolish."

Cordelia embraced her father, grateful to see him in control of his fragile senses. Then Lear finally recognized the Earl of Kent. Blissfully happy to be reunited with his beloved daughter and faithful nobleman, the old king fell back into a deep sleep.

Not far away, Regan's troops had joined with Goneril's and Albany's. The three had arrived to meet with Edmund, who would command the combined forces.

However, the sisters' minds were not on the upcoming war with the French, but on their ongoing battle with each other to win Edmund's love.

As Regan and Goneril argued, Edgar, now clean and dressed as a soldier, sneaked into camp. Finding Albany alone, he asked the duke for permission to challenge Edmund. As proof of Edmund's

KING LEAR

treachery, Edgar offered Albany the letter from Goneril—which plotted his own murder! Albany agreed to call for Edgar when the time was right.

Edmund led the sisters' joint armies into battle. They soundly defeated Cordelia's French forces. Cordelia and Lear were taken prisoner. The Duke of Albany detested the way his wife, Goneril, and sister-in-law, Regan, had treated their father. Albany gave orders that Lear and Cordelia be pardoned. But Edmund had other plans, plans which would put *him* in line for the throne of all Britain. He secretly sent for the prisoners.

Lear and Cordelia were brought before Edmund. Cordelia was defiant. "We are not the first who with best meaning have incurred the worst," she told their captor.

Lear draped his arm around his youngest daughter's shoulder. "Come, let's away to prison," the king said. "We two alone will sing like birds in a cage."

Edmund sent father and daughter to their cell—and handed his captain secret orders to kill them both.

Meanwhile, Edgar returned to Gloucester, whom he had left outside the camp. The young man knelt and at last revealed his identity. The old man, weakened by his injuries and grief for Edmund's treachery, was overpowered by this new joy. His heart burst. The old earl died in his son's arms. Edgar sorrowfully released his father's body and went to the British camp to challenge his treacherous brother.

Albany had already taken up that cause.

The duke called Edmund a traitor. Edmund smugly dared him to find one single person to back up the charge.

"Thou art a traitor, false to thy gods, thy brother, and thy father," a voice called. Edgar marched into the camp, as Regan, Goneril, Albany, and their armies looked on.

Edmund drew his sword. "Back do I toss these treasons to thy head!" The two brothers crossed swords.

Suddenly, Regan collapsed. "Sick, O, sick!" she groaned.

Goneril hid a smile as Regan was carried away. "If not, I'll ne'er trust poison," she muttered.

Edgar and Edmund paid no attention. They fought on, steel clashing against steel. Finally, the elder brother dealt his younger brother a deadly blow. As Edmund collapsed, Goneril threw herself at his feet. Albany held Goneril's letter before her. "Read thine own evil," he snarled at his wife.

Goneril fled to her tent.

A moment later, a frightened servant entered with a bloody knife. Regan was dead of poison at Goneril's hand, the servant reported, and Goneril had stabbed herself.

Faced with his own impending death, Edmund admitted to Albany that he had ordered the murder of Cordelia and Lear. The duke dispatched a messenger with a counterorder at once.

It was too late.

KING LEAR

KING LEAR

"Howl, howl, howl, howl!" King Lear stumbled into the camp. Cordelia's lifeless body lay draped in his arms.

"The heaven's vault should crack!" the distraught king cried. "She's gone forever!" Kent and Albany helped him lay Cordelia on the ground. Lear gently touched his daughter's pale lips and patted her hand. Then he raised his head.

"A plague upon you, murderers, traitors all!" Lear shrieked. The old king was too grieved to live. He wrapped Cordelia's arms around him. "Why should a dog, a horse, a rat, have life, and thou no breath at all?" he whispered. Then, in the cold embrace of the daughter who loved him best, King Lear embraced death himself.

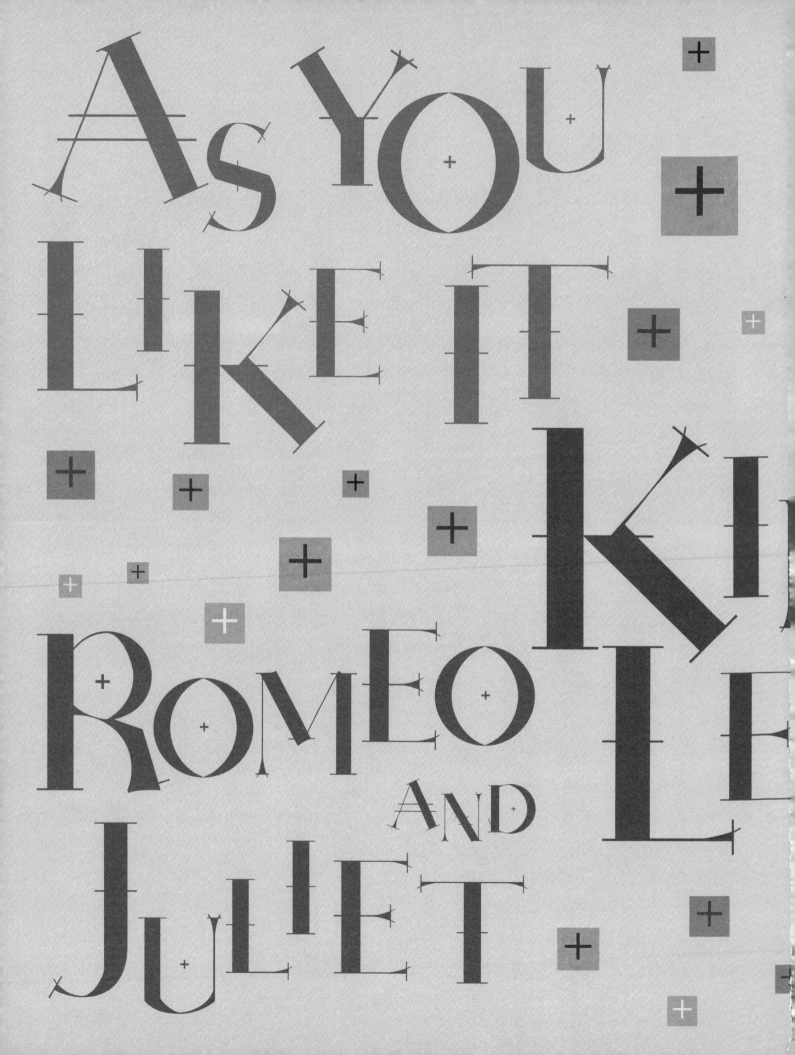